DRUMMING IN THE SKY

DRUMMING IN THE SKY

Poems from 'Stories and Rhymes'

Edited by Paddy Bechely

Illustrated by Priscilla Lamont

BRITISH BROADCASTING CORPORATION

Published by the
British Broadcasting Corporation
35 Marylebone High Street
London W1M 4AA

ISBN 0 563 17900 7

First published 1981
© The British Broadcasting Corporation
and the Contributors 1981

Printed in England
by Jolly & Barber Ltd,
Rugby, Warwickshire

CONTENTS

Acknowledgments Our thanks are due to writers who have given us permission to reprint their copyright material and to the following:

George Allen & Unwin (Publishers) Ltd for *A Lioness* from FIFTY POEMS by Boris Pasternak, *A Small Dragon* from NOTES TO THE HURRYING MAN by Brian Patten and *Oliphaunt* and *There was an Old Dragon* from THE ADVENTURES OF TOM BOMBADIL by J. R. R. Tolkein; American Museum of Natural History for *Navaho Song of a Bear* from NAVAHO TEXTS; Angus and Robertson (UK) Ltd for *Bird*, *Cat Purring*, *Door* and *My Granny is a Witch* (by Arkady Michailov) from AND I DANCE by Keith Bosley; Athaneum Publishers for *The Chant of the Awakening Bulldozers* by Patricia Hubbell; Collins Publishers for *The Dragon Speaks* by C. S. Lewis; Curtis Brown Ltd for *The Greater Cats* by Victoria Sackville-West and *Hullabaloo* by Ursula Moray Williams; Andre Deutsch for *A Busy Day*, *A Cold Fly*, *The Coming of the Phoenix Bird*, *I Share my Bedroom with my Brother*, *If I Were Walking Along the Canal*, *The Longest Journey in the World*, and *One, Two, Three*, by Michael Rosen; Faber and Faber Ltd for *Song of the Ogres* from COLLECTED POEMS by W. H. Auden, *Tom-Cat* by Don Marquis, and *Dibby Dubby Dhu Rose one Midnight* from RUNES AND RHYMES AND TUNES AND CHIMES by George Barker; Granada Publishing Ltd for *come quickly, sitting in a tree*, *now is a ship*, and *here's a little mouse* from COMPLETE POEMS by e. e. cummings, and *Have you heard the sun singing?* from A DISCREET IMMORALITY by John Smith; Hamish Hamilton Ltd for *How to Paint the Portrait of a Bird* by Jacques Prévert from THE FERN ON THE ROCK by Paul Dehn; Harcourt Brace Jovanovich Inc. for *Arithmetic* from THE COMPLETE POEMS OF CARL SANDBURG ©1950 and *Summer Stars* from SMOKE AND STEEL ©1920 by Carl Sandburg; Harper & Row Publishers Inc. for *The Song of the Stars* from KULOSKAP THE MASTER by Charles Godfrey Leland and John Dyneley Prince; William Heinnemann Ltd for *Voices* from UNDERWORLDS by Francis Scarfe; David Higham Associates Ltd for *Cat* by Eleanor Farjeon, *Windows* by Russell Hoban and *Ladybird* by Clive Sansom; Houghton Mifflin Company for *Night Clouds* from THE COMPLETE POETICAL WORKS OF AMY LOWELL ©1955 by Houghton Mifflin Company; Hutchinson Publishing Group Ltd for *The Country Bedroom* from COLLECTED POEMS by Frances Cornford; Hope Leresche & Sayle for *The Fight of the Year* from WATCHWORDS ©1969 by Roger McGough; James MacGibbon and the Literary Executor for *Fairy Story* from COLLECTED POEMS OF STEVIE SMITH published by Allan Lane; Macmillan London and Basingstoke for *Mole* from BROWNJOHN'S BEASTS by Alan Brownjohn and *Cat meets Hedgehog* by Christopher de Cruz from AS LARGE AS ALONE; Harold Matson Company Inc. for *Switch on the Night* ©1955 by Ray Bradbury; Methuen Children's Books for *Bats* and *The Owl* from THE LOST WORLD by Randall Jarrell; Oxford University Press for *Posting Letters* from POSTING LETTERS by Gregory Harrison, *Birds in the Forest*, *Giant Thunder* and *The Toadstool Wood* from THE BLACKBIRD IN THE LILAC by James Reeves and *Out of School* from TOMORROW IS MY LOVE by Hal Summers; Penguin Books Ltd for *The Door* from SELECTED POEMS © Miroslav Holub 1967, translation © Penguin Books 1967, and *Hard Cheese* from JUNIOR VOICES III edited Geoffrey Summerfield by Justin St. John; Sidgwick and Jackson for *India* from THE HUNTER AND OTHER POEMS by W. J. Turner; Smithsonian Institute Press for *Butterfly Song* from MUSIC OF ACOMA, ISLETA, COCHITI AND ZUNI PUEBLOS by Frances Densmore; Society of Authors as representative of the Literary Trustees of Walter de la Mare for *Ice* and *A Song of Enchantment*, and on behalf of Mrs Iris Wise for *Check* and *And it was Windy Weather* by James Stephens; University of Nebraska Press for *Song of the Thunder* and *The Rising of the Buffalo Men* from A SKY CLEARS edited by A. Grove Day; Mrs A. M. Walsh for *'Good-night Mouser'* from THE ROUNDABOUT BY THE SEA by John Walsh; World's Work Ltd for *Esmé on her Brother's Bicycle*, *London City* and *What the Wind Said* from THE PEDALLING MAN by Russell Hoban.

SWITCH ON THE NIGHT

Night switches on the stars and the big white moon; it switches on the glimmer of glow-worms, the dance of moths, the croaking of frogs.

Night switches on the mysterious play of shadows by starlight, moonlight, or lamplight.

CHECK

The Night was creeping on the ground!
She crept and did not make a sound,

Until she reached the tree: and then
She covered it, and stole again

Along the grass beside the wall!
– I heard the rustling of her shawl

As she threw blackness everywhere
Along the sky, the ground, the air,

And in the room where I was hid!
But no matter what she did

To everything that was without
She could not put my candle out!

So I stared at the Night. And she
Stared back solemnly at me!

James Stephens

NIGHT IS HERE

Night is here,
night is here,
dark, dark night.

The stars creep out,
shiny, silver stars,
the stars creep out.

The moon appears,
the moon appears,
white as a snowflake.

The shadows come,
black and grey,
the shadows come.

The sky is dark,
dark, dark, dark,
the sky is dark.

Child author, 8

SWITCH ON THE NIGHT

Once there was a little boy
who didn't like the Night.

He liked
lanterns and lamps
and
torches and tapers
and
beacons and bonfires
and
flashlights and flares.
But he didn't like the Night.

He didn't like light switches at all.
Because light switches turned off
the yellow lamps
the green lamps
the white lamps
the hall lights
the house lights
the lights in all the rooms.
He wouldn't touch a light switch.

And he wouldn't go out to play
after dark.
He was very lonely.
And unhappy.
For he saw, from his window,
the other children playing
on the summer-night lawns.
In and out of the dark and
lamplight ran the children . . .
happily.

But where was our little boy?
Up in his room.
With his lanterns and lamps
and flashlights
and candles and chandeliers.
All by himself.

He liked only the sun.
The yellow sun.
He didn't like
the Night.

When it was time for Mother and Father
to walk around switching off all the
lights . . .
One by one.

One by one.
The porch lights
the parlour lights
the pale lights
the pink lights
the pantry lights
and stairs lights . . .
Then the little boy hid in his bed.

Late at night
his was the only room
with a light
in all the town.

And then one night
With his father away on a trip
And his mother gone to bed early,
The little boy wandered alone,
All alone through the house.

My, how he had the lights blazing!
the parlour lights
and porch lights
the pantry lights
the pale lights
the pink lights
the hall lights
the kitchen lights
even the *attic* lights!
The house looked like it was on fire!

But still the little boy was alone.
While the other children played
on the night lawns.
Laughing.
Far away.

All of a sudden he heard
a rap at a window!
Something dark was there.
A knock at the screen door.
Something dark was there!
A tap at the back porch.
Something dark was there!

And all of a sudden someone said 'Hello!'
And a little girl stood there in the middle of
the white lights, the bright lights,
the hall lights, the small lights,
the yellow lights, the mellow lights.

'My name is Dark,' she said.
And she had dark hair,
and dark eyes,

and wore a dark dress
and dark shoes.
But her face was as white as the moon.
And the light in her eyes
shone like white stars.

'You're lonely,' she said.

'Think what you're missing!
Have you ever thought of
switching on the crickets,
switching on the frogs,
switching on the stars,
and the great big white moon?'

'No,' said the little boy.

'Well, try it,' said Dark.
And they did.

They climbed up and down stairs,
switching on the Night.
Switching on the dark.
Letting the Night live in every room.

Like a frog.
Or a cricket.
Or a star.
Or a moon.

And they switched on the crickets.
And they switched on the frogs.
And they switched on the white, ice-cream moon.

'Oh, I like this!' said the little boy.
'Can I switch on the Night always?'

'Of course!' said Dark, the little girl.
And then she vanished.

And now the little boy is very happy.
He likes the Night.
Now he has a Night-switch instead of a light-switch!
He likes switches now.
He threw away his candles
and flashlights
and lamplights.
And any night in summer that you wish
you can see him

switching on the white moon,
switching on the red stars,
switching on the blue stars,
the green stars, the light stars,
the white stars,
switching on the frogs, the crickets, and Night.

And running in the dark, on the lawns,
with the happy children . . .
Laughing.

Ray Bradbury

ESCAPE AT BEDTIME

The lights from the parlour and kitchen shone out
    Through the blinds and the windows and bars;
And high overhead and all moving about,
    There were thousands of millions of stars.
There ne'er were such thousands of leaves on a tree,
    Nor of people in church or the park,
As the crowds of the stars that looked down upon me,
    And that glittered and winked in the dark.

The Dog, and the Plough, and the Hunter, and all,
    And the star of the sailor, and Mars,
These shone in the sky, and the pail by the wall
    Would be half full of water and stars.
They saw me at last, and they chased me with cries,
    And they soon had me packed into bed;
But the glory kept shining and bright in my eyes,
    And the stars going round in my head.

Robert Louis Stevenson

DIBBY DUBBY DHU ROSE ONE MIDNIGHT

Dibby Dubby Dhu rose one midnight
    to sail his boat in the sky.
He knows that the stars are fishes
    and he even knows why.

Ask: 'Why are the stars fishes?'
    Ask old Dibby Dubby Dhu.
He'll answer: 'Because they are silver
    and swim about in the blue.'

I have seen him standing on tiptoe
    high on the tallest spire
and even on top of the weather cock
    to help him get up higher.

His long fishing line falls UPWARD
    instead of falling down.
And he sees the North Star twinkling far
    below him in the town.

His old fishing boat is anchored fast
    to the very tallest tree.
It bobs and rocks among clouds and church clocks
    as though the sky was sea.

He fishes for stars and birds. And once
    he almost caught the moon,
but his fishing line broke and, alas, he awoke
    just one moment too soon.

George Barker

from THE NIGHT-PIECE TO JULIA

Her Eyes the Glow-worm lend thee,
The Shooting Stars attend thee;
    And the Elves also,
    Whose little eyes glow
Like the sparks of fire, befriend thee.

No *will-o'-the-wisp* mislight thee;
Nor Snake, or Slow-worm bite thee:
    But on, on thy way
    Not making a stay,
Since Ghost there's none to affright thee.

Let not the dark thee cumber;
What though the Moon does slumber?
    The Stars of the night
    Will lend thee their light,
Like Tapers clear without number.

Robert Herrick

DRUMMING IN THE SKY

Sun, moon and stars sing and shout with light in the sky.

Above racing clouds they seem to fly like fiery birds, or beasts with pounding hooves. When thunder rumbles in the clouds, it sounds as though giants are stamping and drumming in the sky.

The voice of the thunder is the voice of gladness, when the storm clouds bring rain and new life to the earth.

HAVE YOU HEARD THE SUN SINGING?

Have you ever heard the sun in the sky
Man have you heard it?
Have you heard it break the black of night
Man have you heard it?

Have you heard it shouting its songs, have you heard
It scorch up the air like a phoenix bird,
Have you heard the sun singing?

from Jazz for five by John Smith

THE SONG OF THE STARS.

We are the stars which sing.
We sing with our light.
We are the birds of fire
We fly across the heaven.

from a Pasamaquoddy Indian song

SUMMER STARS

Bend low again, night of summer stars.
So near you are, sky of summer stars.
So near, a long-arm man can pick off stars,
Pick off what he wants in the sky bowl.
So near you are, summer stars,
So near, strumming, strumming,
    so lazy and hum-strumming.

Carl Sandburg

NIGHT CLOUDS

The white mares of the moon rush along the sky
Beating their golden hoofs upon the glass Heavens;
The white mares of the moon are all standing on their
hind legs
Pawing at the green porcelain doors of the remote
Heavens.
Fly, mares!
Strain your utmost,
Scatter the milky dust of stars,
Or the tiger sun will leap upon you and destroy you
With one lick of his vermilion tongue.

Amy Lowell

from VUKA, XOSA MORNING SONG

The red bull-sun is blazing on the mountains;
He stretches his burning bulk upon the rock-horned
mountains;
He stamps and snorts, and from his flaming nostrils
Red-bellied mists escape and rise.

Francis Carey Slater

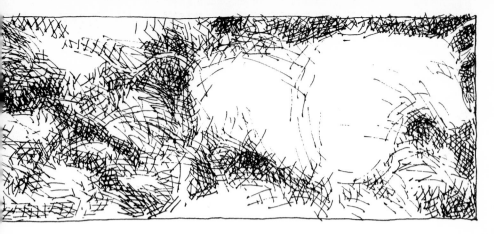

SPELL OF THE RAINGODS

We are the Raingods, we are the clouds,
Gathering and muttering and rumbling together,
Listening to little things praying for wet weather –
        I'm OOM
        I'm BOOM
        and I'm TARAH!

We are howling through the mountains,
We are shrieking through the plain
Billowing and bellowing and ripe with rain –
        He's OOM
        He's BOOM
        and he's TARAH!

We rule the running rivers
And we plump the growing grain
And all the trees are ours for we bring them rain –
        I'm OOM
        I'm BOOM
        and I'm TARAH!

Leslie Norris

SONG OF THE THUNDER

Thonah! Thonah!
There is a voice above,
The voice of thunder,
Within the dark cloud,
Again and again it sounds,
Thonah! Thonah!
Again and again it sounds,
The voice that beautifies the land,
Thonah! Thonah! Thonah! Thonah!

from two Navaho Rain-chants

THUNDER

I hear
the drummers
strike
the sky.

Glenys Van Every

TRANSFORMATIONS

All things change, and from one thing grows another.

Water becomes crystals of ice and snow; snowflakes fall from the sky and cover the earth, as though the sky had broken in little pieces and fallen to the ground; the sun melts the snow and warms the plants, and they put out new leaves and flowers.

We are changed, too, by everything we see and feel around us, and like plants, birds, beasts and fishes, we change and grow with the seasons.

SNOWING

Snowing. Snowing. Snowing.
Woolly petals tossed down
From a tremendous tree in the sky
By a giant hand, the hand
That switches on lightning
And tips down cloudbursts.
I like to think of it that way.

Quiet. Quiet. Quiet.
No noise of traffic in the street.
In the classroom only Miss Nil's voice
Dictating and the rustle of paper.
I am holding my breath in wonder.
I want to cry out 'Look! Look!'
Miss Nil has paused between sentences
And is looking out of the window.
But I suppose she is wondering whether
She'll have to abandon her car and walk home.

Snowing. Snowing. Snowing.
I wish I could go out and taste it.
Feel it nestling against my cheek.
And trickling through my fingers.
The message has come round we are to go home now
Because the buses may stop running.
So the snow has given us a whole hour of freedom.
I pick up fistfuls.
Squeeze them hard and hurl them.

But hurry, the bus is coming
And I want to get home early to look at the garden:

At the holly tree in its polar bear coat;
The cherries with white arms upstretched,
Naked of leaves; the scratchy claw marks
Of birds, and blobs of big pawed dogs.
And I want to make footprints of my own
Where the snow is a blank page for scribbling.
Tea time already. Still the snow comes down.
Migrating moths, millions and millions
Dizzying down out of the darkening sky.

Mother draws the curtains.
Why couldn't they stay open?
Now I can't watch the secretive birds
Descending, the stealthy army invading.
What does the roof look like
Covered with slabs of cream?
How high are the heaps on window ledges?
Tomorrow the snow may have begun to melt away.
O, why didn't I look more
While there was still time?

Olive Dove

SNOW AND SUN

White bird, featherless,
Flew from Paradise,
Pitched on the castle wall;

Along came Lord Landless,
Took it up handless,
And rode away horseless to the King's white hall.

Author unknown

ICE

The North Wind sighed:
And in a trice
What was water
Now is ice.

What sweet rippling
Water was
Now bewitched is
Into glass:

White and brittle
Where is seen
The prisoned milfoil's
Tender green;

Clear and ringing
With sun aglow,
Where the boys sliding
And skating go.

Now furred's each stick
And stalk and blade
With crystals out of
Dewdrops made.

Worms and ants
Flies, snails and bees
Keep close house guard,
Lest they freeze;

O, with how sad
And solemn an eye
Each fish stares up
Into the sky

In dread lest his
Wide watery home
At night shall solid
Ice become.

Walter de la Mare

SNOW

The sky is heavy and very pale,
The sky is full of flakes,
The sky breaks into little pieces,
And falls curling to the ground,
The ground is covered
Just like the sky.

Stephen Ward, 7

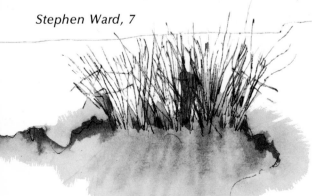

WINTER IS HERE

Clouds sag.
Puddles are glass.
Naked elms – cities of the rook – forsaken.
Red hips where the wild rose flushed.
Cow parsley dried brown.
A few seeds not shed.
Oo! it's cold.
My breath walks before me.
My fingers feel fat.
Snow. Yes, it really is snow at last
Dizzying down like woolly moths
Without a sound.
I want to make a noise.
I want to call everyone out.
I want to shout 'Look, winter is here!'

Olive Dove

THE FIGHT OF THE YEAR

'And there goes the bell for the third month
and Winter comes out of its corner looking groggy
Spring leads with a left to the head
followed by a sharp right to the body
    daffodils
    primroses
    crocuses
    snowdrops
    lilacs
    violets
    pussywillow

Winter can't take much more punishment
and Spring shows no signs of tiring
    tadpoles
    squirrels
    baalambs
    badgers
    bunny rabbits
    mad march hares
    horses and hounds
Spring is merciless

Winter won't go the full twelve rounds
    bobtail clouds
    scallywaggy winds
    the sun
    a pavement artist
    in every town
A left to the chin
and Winter's down!
    1 tomatoes
    2 radish
    3 cucumber
    4 onions
    5 beetroot
    6 celery
    7 and any
    8 amount
    9 of lettuce
    10 for dinner
Winter's out for the count
Spring is the winner!'

Roger McGough

THE TOUGH GUY OF LONDON

Seen from within a heated room,
On a sunny February afternoon,
London looks like
Any other summer's day.

Step out in only
Your shirt and trousers
And, even with a black belt in karate,
An invisible tough guy
With blimey cold hands and feet,
Punches you
Smack on the nose
Straight back in.

Kojo Gyinaye Kyei

COME, QUICKLY

come quickly come
run run
with me now
jump shout (laugh
dance cry

sing) for it's Spring

– irrevocably;
and in
earth sky trees
: every
where a miracle arrives

(yes)

from a longer poem by e.e. cummings

30

IN THE BRIGHT AIR

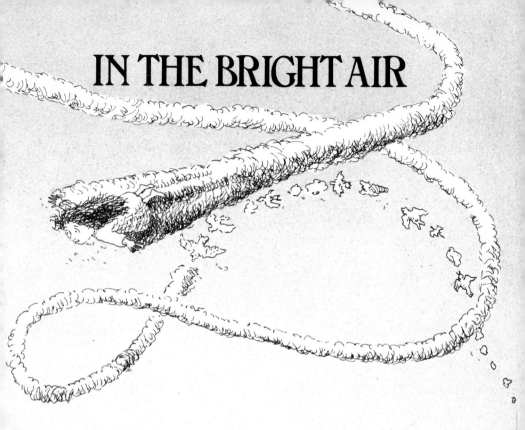

In the bright air of evening, by moonlight or starlight, the dark shapes of bats whirl and dance.

In morning sunlight butterflies skip and fall like white petals, and small birds sing and fly. What would it be like if we could grow wings, if we could float weightless, feeling the air like water flowing past us, looking down on rooftops and treetops, and all familiar things very small and far below, their sounds very faint and distant too?

The way people fly is by 'plane – sitting in the sky, eating and drinking, and looking down at the wrinkling waves of the sea and fields like check tablecloths. That is how people travel the roads of the air, bumpy roads rising and falling, but roads made of nothing.

BATS

A bat is born
Naked and blind and pale.
His mother makes a pocket of her tail
And catches him. He clings to her long fur
By his thumbs and toes and teeth.
And then the mother dances through the night
Doubling and looping, soaring, somersaulting –
Her baby hangs on underneath.
All night, in happiness, she hunts and flies.
Her high sharp cries
Like shining needlepoints of sound
Go out into the night and, echoing back,
Tell her what they have touched.
She hears how far it is, how big it is,
Which way it's going:
She lives by hearing.
The mother eats the moths and gnats she catches
In full flight; in full flight

The mother drinks the water of the pond
She skims across. Her baby hangs on tight.
Her baby drinks the milk she makes him
In moonlight or starlight, in mid-air.
Their single shadow, printed on the moon
Or fluttering across the stars,
Whirls on all night; at daybreak
The tired mother flaps home to her rafter.
The others are all there.
They hang themselves up by their toes,
They wrap themselves in their brown wings.
Bunched upside-down, they sleep in air.
Their sharp ears, their sharp teeth, their quick sharp faces
Are dull and slow and mild.
All the bright day, as the mother sleeps,
She folds her wings about her sleeping child.

Randall Jarrell

HOW TO ADDRESS A BAT

Arymouse, Arymouse, fly over my head,
And you shall have a crust of bread;
And when I brew and when I bake,
You shall have a piece of my wedding-cake.

Traditional

BUTTERFLY SONG

Butterfly, butterfly, butterfly, butterfly.
Oh look, see it hovering among the flowers,
It is like a baby trying to walk, and not knowing how to go . . .

THE DREAM OF THE CABBAGE-CATERPILLARS

There was no magic spell:
    all of us, sleeping,
dreamed the same dream – a dream
    that's ours for the keeping.

In sunbeam or dripping rain,
    sister by brother,
we once roamed with glee
    the leaves which our mother

laid us and left us on,
    browsing our fill
of green cabbage, fresh cabbage,
    thick cabbage, until

in the hammocks we hung
    on the garden wall
came sleep, and the dream
    that changed us all –

we had left our soft bodies
    the munching, the crawling,
to skim through the clear air, like
    white petals falling!

Now, true love by true love,
    we skip high as towers
and dip not to cabbage leaves
    but trembling bright flowers.

Libby Houston.

BIRDS

A bird flies and has wings
And it certainly sings

A bird when it sings is always certain.
It sings and sings about certain things,
Like flying and having wings
Or being only a bird in a tree
and free.

Free is when you are being certain
And wanting to sing certainly
About certain things.

A bird is free and certainly sings.
It sings and sings about flying and having wings
Or being always a certain thing
When it is only a bird in a tree
Singing certainly
And free.

Ray Fabrizio

BIRD SIPS WATER

Bird
sips water
drips music
throwing back its head

throw back your head
turn the rain
into a song
and you will fly

Keith Bosley

BIRD AND BOY

So you want to fly. Why?
  You haven't any feathers.
Do you think it's good fun
  Being out in all weathers?
Said Bird to Boy.

You haven't any wings,
  You can't build a nest.
Why aren't you satisfied.
  With the things you do best?
Said Bird to Boy.

What would it be like?
  A sky full of boys,
Their arms flapping, their big feet –
  And the noise!
Said Bird to Boy.

Have you ever tried perching
  In some old tree
When it's snowing? It's not funny,
  Believe me!
Said Bird to Boy.

Be comfortable, do your own thing,
  Your skateboard, your bike,
Your football, all the other
  Things you like.
Why try to fly?
  Stay out of the sky,
Said Bird to Boy.

Yes, you're right, I can't just
  Flap my arms and fly.

But I dream about it often,
   Winging through the sky,
Above the houses, the streets.
   I'd like to try.
Said Boy to Bird.

Leslie Norris

FLYING BOY

I woke early this morning,
Feeling awkward in my bed.
I rubbed my sleepy eyes a bit
And shook my sleepy head,

And wondered in a sleepy way
Why I'd suddenly grown wings;
They'd grown from my shoulders –
Long feathery things.

I tried them out carefully
And fluttered to the stairs
And glided like a butterfly
Above the bannisters.

My mum was in the kitchen.
I flew above her head.
'Am I an angel, Mum?' I asked.
'Eat your breakfast,' she said.

'Am I a bird?' I asked her.
She said, 'What silly talk.
Whoever heard of a bird that could
Use a knife and fork?
Are you going to fly to school?
Wouldn't you rather walk?'

My friends below me walked to school
Like a swarm of tiny bees,
But I flew over the rooftops,
I flew over the trees,

I soared through the cloudbanks,
Spun round the tallest towers.
I can dive and I can loop,
I've been practising for hours.

But now the lights are coming out,
The pale stars shine.
The cars take all their drivers home
And I must fly to mine.

All day long I've owned the air
And beat my wings through the sky.
The little streets were far below,
Each little house a toy,
And all the people, looking up,
Waved to the flying boy.

Leslie Norris

FLYING

Flying
   He saw the earth flat as a plate,
   As if there were no hills, as if houses
   Were only roofs, as if the trees
   Were only the leaves that covered
   The treetops. He could see the shadows
   The clouds cast when they sailed over fields,
   He saw the river like the silver track
   Left by a snail, and roads narrow as ribbons.

He could not see Mickey French next door
In bed with a cold, nor his two sisters
Playing Happy Families as they watched
The television. He could not see his kitten.

Flying,
    He felt the air almost as hard as water
    When he spread his fingers against it,
    He felt it cool against his face, he felt
    His hair whipped about. He felt weightless
    As if he were hollow, he felt the sun
    Enormously bright and warm on his back,
    He felt his eyes watering. He felt
    The small, moist drops the clouds held.

    He could not feel the grass, he could not
    Feel the rough stones of the garden wall.
    He could not remember the harsh, dry bark
    Of the apple tree against his knees.

Flying,
    He could hear the wind hissing, the note
    Changed when he moved his head. He heard
    His own voice when he sang. Very faintly,
    He heard the school bus as it grumbled
    Past the church, he thought he could hear
    The voices of the people as they shouted
    In amazement when they saw him swoop and glide.

    He could not hear birds sing, nor the chalk
    Squeak against the blackboard, nor the mower,
    As it whirred along, nor the clock tick.
    He could not hear bacon sizzle in the pan,
    He could not hear his friend calling him.

Leslie Norris

FLYING TO INDIA

And so we climbed inside the plane,
Sam, Alice and I,
to sit in the sky – to fly
all the way over the side of the world
to India
was our adventure.

FASTEN YOUR SEAT-BELTS!
They fastened the door,
the engines behind us,
the runways before,
and, lurching gently,
we started to creep
as low as a moth
on the kitchen floor –
to wait our turn
where, large and small,
as if it was apparatus-day
in a giant machines' school hall,
the aeroplanes queue
for the take-off run,
one by one.

The Jumbo's gone –
and now it's us!
Like a boiling kettle
at the whistle
the engines screaming,
we're off! We're running
the wide white road
like a galloping horse
the last fence ahead,
faster and faster,

so heavy inside
you could feel her gather up
all of her power
to hurl her metal
and all her load,
clumsy and loud,
at the thin light air –
nothing can stop us!
Up goes the nose,
and the people in front of us
tilting backwards
nearly on top of us,
things bump and jolt,
and through the window –
look, there's a roof,
and Windsor Castle!
Magical racehorse, horse of metal,
far did your proud jump go!

They brought us strange food,
black-haired ladies
in blood-red blouses
with smiling faces,
and tiny paper packets of pepper,
salt, milk powder, toothpicks and sugar –
we picked and poked, we sprinkled and stirred,
and ate,
and drank:
enchanted food
it might have been,
for we saw what we had never seen.

For when I looked out,
I saw the sea
Stretch like a fan,
edging the land
far, far below, and nothing between –
I saw England's roots, pale roots of sand
going down deep through the rich blue water,
and all the waves between England and France
so long and still,
you could count them all.

Suddenly we bucked and stumbled,
I was afraid, I thought aeroplanes never trembled
What's happened?
A wisp like a ghost brushed by –
it was just a bump in the road of the sky!
Thick air and thin, air rising and falling:
strange road,
made of so much nothing!

Overhead
it was brilliant blue –
but under us now
there began to gather
a fat froth, milky and thick, until
on an endless carpet of cotton-wool,
we were alone, so small,
Like a lonely fly, upstairs in an empty room –
then we dipped through.

Down through the ceiling we came, to a land
where tiny square houses stood neat in a row,
no bigger than dolls' houses for dolls,
by a road like a ruler,
and coming and going,
matchbox lorries, pin-men's cars,
none of them knowing
that we could see!
We stopped for breath, it was Germany.

Night poured round us
and on we went,
in black, to Rome,
where the floor was swept.
The engines hurt, they roared at our ears so loud –
and at last we slept.

Somewhere behind us, far away,
  our street lay
    tucked in that shadow-bed
  of night –
but though the dark held on to our tail,
  we ran ahead,
    ran, till we overtook time, meeting the next day
      half-way, straight for the sun's big apricot,
        and first for us the golden light,
          showing the way!

  O we were flying above a brown country:
    brown rocks, brown sand, and not a tree
      or field or town that we could see,
        but a thin road, going on and on
          through the dreary deserts of Iran.
        We grew weary, bored, tired,
            sitting so long
              stuck in the air –
        How much longer till we get there?

Deserts and mountains passed,
                and then, at last,
  the world spread open a vast
yellowy greeny blue check table-cloth,
bunches of villages set among the squares,
  and the pilot, his voice all fuzzy,
      announced where we were –
                it was India!

  Lovely were the clouds
    the day put up to greet us,
      white twists of barley-sugar,
        curly locks of hair –
it was dinner-time when we landed there.

Now over fields with wavy edges
and felt-pen hills with furry faces
under a cloud like a scarf we flew –
it was brown beneath white beneath blue –
when suddenly, higher than us, one after
another, above the cloud, we saw,
like planets unknown to the world below,
dazzling black rocks and bright snow –
     peaks of the giant Himalayas,
shining, as if they'd come out to see us!

  This was the land our ticket promised,
      we came in to land –
           our friends were there to meet us –
  Look! There's Chris and Moraig and Hamish!
  We touched the ground,
      we laughed and shouted and ran
           in the fresh wind and the warm sun!

  Empty, forgotten,
  the magical horse lay dumb.

Libby Houston

THEY GO BUT SOFTLY

There are creatures who move over the earth so quietly that they make no sound to our ears, but although some of them are very small and nearly silent, and disturb the world around them very little, they pursue their quiet purposes with the same energy as larger, noisier beasts.

UPON THE SNAIL

She goes but softly, but she goeth sure
She stumbles not as stronger creatures do;
Her journey's shorter, so she may endure
Better than they which do much further go.

John Bunyan

MOLE

To have to be a mole?

It is like, in a way,
being a little car driven
in the very dark,
                    owned
by these endless-
ly tunnelling paws and small
eyes that are good, only,
for the underground.

What can you know of me, this
warm black engine of
busying velvet?

Soft mounds of new, pale
earth like finely-flaked ash
tell you just about where
my country is, but
do you ever see
                    me?

Alan Brownjohn

'GOOD-NIGHT MOUSER!'

'Good-night, Mouser!'
The front door closes,
The bolt slides home,
And Mouser hops down into the garden,
A cat unwanted, alone.

The late-night neighbour,
Hurrying along
Click-clack on the empty street,
Feels a sudden fur at his feet.
Wondering he bends,
And Mouser winds about him,
Furring him,
Purring him
Most pleadingly,
For even in the dark, Mouser knows all his friends.
But the neighbour rises and feels for his key:
'Good night, Mouser!
Run away now and play!'
And Mouser wanders away.

All the long night he'll stray
Through empty garden, or waste and thorny patch,
Nosing at a pebble or a snail
In the flower-bed;
His ears straining to catch
The squeak of a fallen fledgling, not yet dead;
His paw ready to snatch
At the scuttering rat,
Or the beaded mouse with the flickering tail.
All the long night, prowling and prying,
Around the cold roots of the thorns;

Or sometimes just lying
In a tuft of grass,
Just lying in wait, no more.
But when daylight dawns
He is back at the door –
Back with his doorstep offering of rat or mouse;

And he sits with uplifted chin,
Endlessly patient, watching the house
Watching for the twitch of the curtain,
Waiting for the slide of the bolt,
And the voice that cries, 'Come in!'

Stay in tonight, Mouser!
Quick, up the stairs before others can see!
No longer alone,
NOT a cat-without-a-home,
Stay warm in my bed with me!

John Walsh

HOW SOFT A CATERPILLAR STEPS

How soft a caterpillar steps,
I find one on my hand . . .

Emily Dickinson

LADYBIRD

Tiniest of turtles!
Your shining back
Is a shell of orange
With spots of black.

How trustingly you walk
Across this land
Of hairgrass and hollows
That is my hand.

Your small wire legs,
So frail, so thin,
Their touch is swansdown
Upon my skin.

There! break out
Your wings and fly
No tenderer creature
Beneath the sky.

Clive Sansom

CLOCK-A-CLAY

In the cowslip pips I lie,
Hidden from the buzzing fly,
While green grass beneath me lies,
Pearled with dew like fishes' eyes,
Here I lie, a clock-a-clay,
Waiting for the time of day.

While grassy forest quakes surprise,
And the wild wind sobs and sighs,
My gold home rocks as like to fall,
On its pillar green and tall;
When the pattering rain drives by
Clock-a-clay keeps warm and dry.

Day by day and night by night,
All the week I hide from sight;
In the cowslip pips I lie,
In rain and dew still warm and dry;
Day and night, and night and day,
Red, black-spotted clock-a-clay.

My home shakes in wind and showers,
Pale green pillar topped with flowers,
Bending at the wild wind's breath,
Till I touch the grass beneath;
Here I live, lone clock-a-clay,
Watching for the time of day.

John Clare

A LITTLE MOUSE

A little mouse running
its feet tapping lightly upon the ground
its ears bright pink in the sunlight
its coat thick and grey
its tail long and curly
its eyes straining and looking for food.

Ruth Bechely, 8

HERE'S A LITTLE MOUSE . . .

here's a little mouse) and
what does he think about, i
wonder as over this
floor (quietly with

bright eyes) drifts (nobody
can tell because
Nobody knows, or why
jerks Here &, here,
gr(oo)ving the room's Silence) this like
a littlest
poem a
(with wee ears and see?

tail frisks)
          (gonE)

e.e. cummings

THE OWL

A shadow is floating through the moonlight.
Its wings don't make a sound.
Its claws are long, its beak is bright.
Its eyes try all the corners of the night.

It calls and calls: all the air swells and heaves
And washes up and down like water.
The ear that listens to the owl believes
In death. The bat beneath the eaves,

The mouse beside the stone are still as death –
The owl's air washes them like water.
The owl goes back and forth inside the night,
And the night holds its breath.

Randall Jarrell

WHISKY FRISKY

Whisky Frisky, hipperty hop,
Up he goes to the tree top!
Whirly, twirly, round and round,
Down he scampers to the ground.
Furly, curly, what a tail,
Tall as a feather, broad as a sail.
Where's his supper? In the shell.
Snappy, cracky, out it fell.

Traditional

THE SERPENT

Wake the serpent not – lest he
Should not know the way to go –
Let him crawl which yet lies sleeping
Through the deep grass of the meadow!
Not a bee shall hear him creeping,
Not a mayfly shall awaken
From its cradling blue-bell shaken,
Not the starlight as he's sliding
Through the grass with silent gliding.

P. B. Shelley

GRASS SNAKE

We waited so long to see,
Sitting under a birch tree.

She came at last hithery, thithery,
Sliding, gliding, swiftly, slithery.

Her great eyes gold,
Unlidded, bold.

A little afraid of her?
Yes, we were.

But she was so beautiful and dignified
That, soon as born, our fears died.

And she noticed us less than stones,
Heather, grass and rabbit bones.

Olive Dove

SNAKE MOVING

With undulations
From side to side
Through tall grasses
With footless stride
I glide.

While my double tongue
Like twin sticks
Is feeling its way around
As it flicks
And licks.

Olive Dove

CAT PURRING

Cat
purring

four furry paws
walking

delicate-
ly

    between
flower stems
stalking

butter-
flies.

Keith Bosley

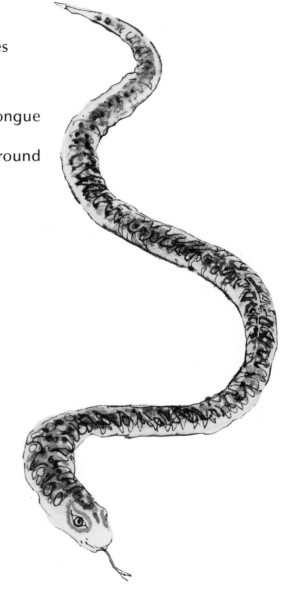

CAT MEETS HEDGEHOG

Cat sees round prickly ball
On the lawn.
It sees all pads on paw.
And then it touches,
And brings its paw away quickly.
Ouch it hurt.
Cat wonders what is it,
Something strange.
Cat pushes it with its paw.
Hurts more.
Cat runs away and thinks to itself,
Not going there again.
Cat watches prickly ball from bush.
Prickly ball changes from round to long.
Four legs come out. A head comes out,
And it starts to move.
Cat gets more scared.
Cat runs far away,
And hopes it sees nothing like that again.

Christopher de Cruz

CLAWS AND PAWS

Here are hunters and chasers, barkers and growlers, with sharp teeth and claws and glowing eyes.

Here are great beasts whose tread makes the ground tremble and who carry formidable horns, and here are giants who move quietly and whose ways are gentle.

THE WIRE-HAIRED FOX-TERRIER

I am a blithe
    Fox Terrier
And nobody can be
     Merrier
     Or friskier
     Or whiskrier
Or should that be whisKERRier?
Than a wire-haired
    Fox Terrier
I am a great
    Cat chaser
And garden tennisball
     Racer
    Nosey Parker
    Noisy barker
And middle of the lawn bone-burier
I'm a wire-haired
    Fox Terrier.

I am a rough
    Rat worrier
And bouncing scoot and
      Scurrier
    Out of mischief
    Into mischief
Stream-paddler and stick-carrier
I'm a wire-haired
    Fox Terrier.
At night I am
    A sleeper
And nobody can sleep
    Deeper
    Or snoozier
    Or cosier
When the frost outside gets frozier
Than a tired
    Fox Terrier

Leslie Norris

CAT

Cat!
Scat!
Atter her, atter her,
Sleeky flatterer,
Spitfire chatterer,
Scatter her, scatter her,
Off her mat!
Wuff!
Wuff!
Treat her rough!
Git her, git her,
Whiskery spitter!
Catch her, catch her,
Green-eyed scratcher!
Slathery
Slithery
Hisser,
Don't miss her!

Run till you're dithery,
    Hithery
    Thithery
    Pfitts! Pfitts!
    How she spits!
    Spitch! Spatch!
    Can't she scratch!
Scritching the bark
Of the sycamore-tree,
She's reached her ark
And's hissing at me
    Pfitts! Pfitts!
    Wuff! Wuff!
    Scat,
    Cat!
    That's
    That!

Eleanor Farjeon

TOM-CAT

At midnight in the alley
A tom-cat comes to wail,
And he chants the hate of a million years
As he swings his snaky tail.

Malevolent, bony, brindled,
Tiger and devil and bard,
His eyes are coals from the middle of Hell
And his heart is black and hard.

He twists and crouches and capers
And bares his curved sharp claws,
And he sings to the stars of the jungle nights,
E're cities were, or laws.

Beast from a world primeval
He and his leaping clan,
When the blotched red moon leers over the roofs,
Give voice to their scorn of man.

He will lie on a rug tomorrow
And lick his silky fur,
And veil the brute in his yellow eyes
And play he's tame, and purr.

But at midnight in the alley
He will crouch again and wail,
And beat the time for his demon's song
With the swing of his demon's tail.

Don Marquis

ALLEY CAT

A bit of jungle in the street
He goes on velvet toes,
And slinking through the shadows, stalks
Imaginary foes.

Esther Valck Georges

INDIA

They hunt, the velvet tigers in the jungle,
The spotted jungle full of shapeless patches –
Sometimes they're leaves, sometimes they're
    hanging flowers,
Sometimes they're hot gold patches of the sun:
They hunt, the velvet tigers in the jungle!

What do they hunt by glimmering pools of water,
By the round silver Moon, the Pool of Heaven –
In the striped grass, amid the barkless trees –
The stars scattered like eyes of beasts above them!

What do they hunt, their hot breath scorching insects;
Insects that blunder blindly in the way,
Vividly fluttering – they also are hunting,
Are glittering with a tiny ecstasy!

The grass is flaming and the trees are growing,
The very mud is gurgling in the pools,
Green toads are watching, crimson parrots flying,
Two pairs of eyes meet one another glowing –
They hunt, the velvet tigers in the jungle.

W. J. Turner

THE GREATER CATS

The greater cats with golden eyes
Stare out between the bars.
Deserts are there, and different skies,
And night with different stars.

Victoria Sackville-West

A LIONESS

A lioness the people facing,
Relentlessly the floorboards pacing
And turning on her only track
First there, then back, then there, then back,
Is driven by her very raging
When brushing at the iron caging;
The barrier pattern stark and black,
Is moving with her there and back.

from The Zoo by Boris Pasternak, translated by Lydia Pasternak

ELEPHANT

Grey and clumbery,
big and lumbery,
swishing his great long nose.

Clumfing and lumfing
bumping and humping,
that's the way the elephant goes.

Jane Barber, 8

OLIPHAUNT

Grey as a mouse,
Big as a house,
Nose like a snake;
I make the earth shake
As I tramp through the grass;
Trees crack as I pass.
With horns in my mouth
I walk in the South,
Flapping big ears.
Beyond count of years
I stump round and round,
Never lie on the ground,
Not even to die,
Oliphaunt am I,
Biggest of all,
Huge, old and tall.
If ever you'd met me,
You wouldn't forget me.
If you never do
You won't think I'm true;
But old Oliphaunt am I,
And I never lie.

J. R. R. Tolkien

NAVAHO SONG OF A BEAR

There is danger where I move my feet.
I am a whirlwind. There is danger where I move my feet.
I am a gray bear.
When I walk, where I step lightning flies from me.
Where I walk, one to be feared.
Where I walk, long life.
One to be feared I am.
There is danger where I walk.

THE RISING OF THE BUFFALO MEN

I rise, I rise,
I, whose tread makes the earth to rumble.
I rise, I rise,
I, who shakes his mane when angered.
I rise, I rise,
I, whose horns are sharp and curved.

Osage Indian song

PRAISE GOD FOR THE ANIMALS

Praise God for the animals:
for the colours of them,
for the stripes and spots of them,
for the patches and plains of them,
their claws and paws.

Lynn Warren, 8

HERE BE DRAGONS

Scaily, flaily-tailed beasts, breathing fire, hatched from eggs, growing from worm to serpent.

In ancient times in Britain and China, and in other lands too, dragons were believed to be creatures of life-giving power, and in some places they are still.

At other times and in other places, dragons were wicked; they lived hidden in caves, forests and deep wells; they ate sheep and cattle and children; they loved gold, and guarded hoards of treasure in their dark dens.

Where are dragons now? Have they diminished in size and power to become tiny black and gold creatures creeping out of a pond on a night of thunderstorm?

THE DRAGON WITH A BIG NOSE

The dragon
with a big nose
and twelve toes
on each foot
eats flies
and mince pies

and sometimes
when he's very bad
whole towns
upside down

streets and houses
shops and churches
schools and fact'ries
undergrounds

swallows them all
quite whole
and spits out the glass fast
treading very carefully
somewhere else
going away.

No one's ever seen him coming
they can't see him leave.
No one's ever seen him anyway
.....................except me!

Kathy Henderson

THE DRAGON OF WANTLEY

This dragon had two furious wings
One upon each shoulder,
With a sting in his tail as long as a flail
Which made him bolder and bolder.
He had long claws, and in his jaws
Four and forty teeth of iron,
With a hide as tough as any buff
Which did him round environ.

Have you not heard how the Trojan horse
Held seventy men in his belly?
This dragon wasn't quite so big
But very near I'll tell ye.
Devoured he poor children three
That could not with him grapple,
And at one sup he ate them up
As you would eat an apple.

All sorts of cattle this dragon did eat
Some say he ate up trees,
And that the forests sure he would
Devour by degrees.
For houses and churches were to him
    geese and turkeys
He ate all, and left none behind
But some stones, good sirs, that he
    couldn't crack
Which on the hills you'll find.

from an English folk song

DRAGON

A dragon has come
To the side of my bed.
How did it get in?
It is, of course, red.

'O, jawsome, clawsome,
Scaily, flaily tailed beast
Do you want me
For a midnight feast?'

Turns off its fire.
Turns off its smoke.
'Dragon, did you hear
The words I spoke?'

Eyes me like my dog
When he sits up to beg
Then ambles away.
IT'S LAID AN EGG!

Olive Dove

A SMALL DRAGON

I've found a small dragon in the woodshed.
Think it must have come from deep inside a forest
because it's damp and green and leaves
are still reflecting in its eyes.

I fed it on many things, tried grass,
the roots of stars, hazel-nut and dandelion,
but it stared up at me as if to say, I need
foods you can't provide.

It made a nest among the coal,
not unlike a bird's but larger,
it is out of place here
and is quite silent.

If you believed in it I would come
hurrying to your house to let you share my wonder,
but I want instead to see
if you yourself will pass this way.

Brian Patten

MY NEWTS

One night in thunder,
Two newts came to our back door to shelter
From the torrential rain and gusty wind;
I found them there when the rain had passed.
I caught them and kept them.
They are small and squirm when they are picked up.
Their stomachs and breasts are orange and black,
Pulsing with life.
They have four webbed feet and long shiny tails;
They are elegantly exact when they swim.

Out of the thunder night,
Came my black and orange dragons.

Clarissa Hinsley

THERE WAS AN OLD DRAGON

There was an old dragon under grey stone;
his red eyes blinked as he lay alone.
His joy was dead and his youth spent,
he was knobbed and wrinkled, and his limbs bent
in the long years to his gold chained;
in his heart's furnace the fire waned.
To his belly's slime gems stuck thick,
silver and gold he would snuff and lick:
he knew the place of the least ring
beneath the shadow of his black wing.
Of thieves he thought on his hard bed,
and dreamed that on their flesh he fed,
their bones crushed, and their blood drank:
his ears drooped and his breath sank.
Mail-rings rang. He heard them not.
A voice echoed in his deep grot:
a young warrior with a bright sword
called him forth to defend his hoard.
His teeth were knives, and of horn his hide,
but iron tore him, and his flame died.

from The Hoard by J. R. R. Tolkien

THE DRAGON SPEAKS

'Now I keep watch on the gold in my rock cave
In a country of stones: old, deplorable dragon,
Watching my hoard. In winter night the gold
Freezes through toughest scales my cold belly.
The jagged crowns and twisted cruel rings
Knobbly and icy are old dragon's bed.

Often I wish I hadn't eaten my wife,
Though worm grows not to dragon till he eat worm.
She could have helped me, watch and watch about,
Guarding the hoard. Gold would have been the safer.
I could uncoil my weariness at times and take
A little sleep, sometimes when she was watching.

Last night under the moonset a fox barked,
Woke me. Then I knew I had been sleeping.
Often an owl flying over the country of stones
Startles me, and I think I must have slept.
Only a moment. That very moment a man
Might have come out of the cities, stealing,
    to get my gold.'

from The Dragon Speaks by C. S. Lewis

FROM HIS NOSE, CLOUDS HE BLOWS

There are old giants of earth and sky whose upheavals shape the land: their voices thunder in the skies, their footsteps set the mountains trembling, they sleep in volcanoes and fight in the storm clouds. There are cowardly giants – big but not brave – in fairy tales.

And there are ogres – these are the dangerous ones – greedy and lazy, deceitful and cruel, they do not understand honesty, loyalty, generosity or friendship.

It is ogres that giant-killers and their friends go out to fight, and must go on fighting, though thousands of years pass, until the world is rid of them.

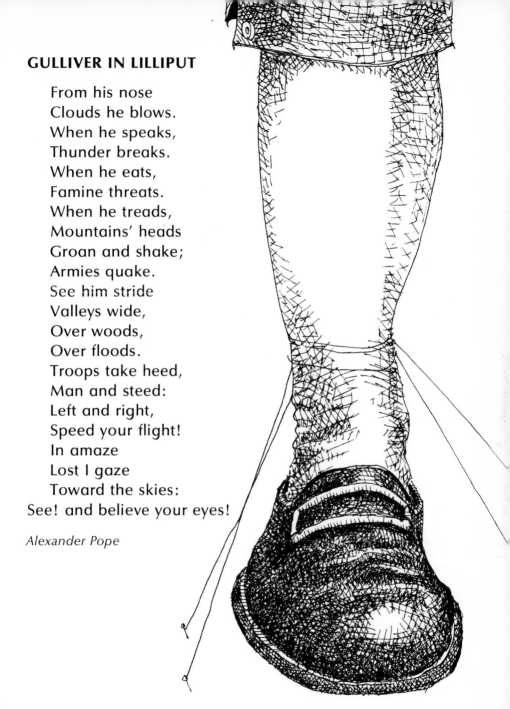

GULLIVER IN LILLIPUT

From his nose
Clouds he blows.
When he speaks,
Thunder breaks.
When he eats,
Famine threats.
When he treads,
Mountains' heads
Groan and shake;
Armies quake.
See him stride
Valleys wide,
Over woods,
Over floods.
Troops take heed,
Man and steed:
Left and right,
Speed your flight!
In amaze
Lost I gaze
Toward the skies:
See! and believe your eyes!

Alexander Pope

from FRODGE-DOBBULUM

Did you ever see Giant Frodge-dobbulum,
With his double great-toe and his double great-thumb?

Did you ever hear Giant Frodge-dobbulum
Saying *Fa-fe-fi* and *fo-faw-fum*?

He shakes the earth as he walks along,
As deep as the sea, as far as Hong-Kong!

He is a giant and no mistake,
With teeth like the prongs of a garden rake.

W. B. Rands

THE GIANT FOLLDEROWE

Who uses a mountain as his bed
and on the soft clouds rests his head
and never feels he's fully fed?
           The Giant Follderowe.
Whose feet are cold, and white as rice,
who dipped them in the ocean twice
and made the North and South Poles ice?
           The Giant Follderowe.
Whose hand can hide the noonday sun
and make you think that night has come,
whose age is a thousand and ninety-one?
           The Giant Follderowe.
Who's sleeping near the frozen lakes,
snoring and rumbling until the earth shakes?
What's going to happen when he awakes,
           The Giant Follderowe?

Leslie Norris

GIANT THUNDER

Giant Thunder, striding home,
Wonders if his supper's done.

'Hag wife, hag wife, bring me my bones!'
'They are not done,' the old hag moans.

'Not done? Not done?' the giant roars
And heaves his old wife out of doors.

Cries he, 'I'll have them, cooked or not!'
But overturns the cooking pot.

He flings the burning coals about;
See how the lightning flashes out!

Upon the gale the old hag rides,
The cloudy moon for terror hides.

All the world with thunder quakes;
Forest shudders, mountain shakes;
From the cloud the rainstorm breaks;
Village ponds are turned to lakes;
Every living creature wakes.

Hungry Giant, lie you still!
Stamp no more from hill to hill –
Tomorrow you shall have your fill.

James Reeves

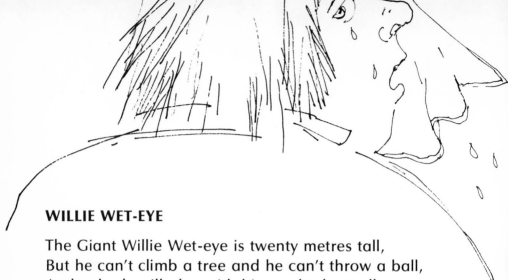

WILLIE WET-EYE

The Giant Willie Wet-eye is twenty metres tall,
But he can't climb a tree and he can't throw a ball,
And nobody will play with him, nobody at all.
    Wipe your eyes, Willie, wipe away your tears.

His old uncle Thundervoice is grumbling aloud,
His fierce aunt Wintercold is black as a cloud,
They aren't proud of Willie, not at all proud.
    Wipe your eyes, Willie, wipe away your tears.

His grandfather, old Mountainous, ate twenty men for tea,
His mother's cousin Blottingpad, drank half the Irish Sea,
But wailing Willie Wet-eye is afraid of you and me.
    Wipe your eyes, Willie, wipe away your tears.

His mother feeds him oatmeal out of a wooden tub,
His father worries over him and gives his head a rub,
But poor Willie Wet-eye, all he can do is blub.
    Wipe your eyes, Willie, wipe away your tears.

When the summer comes again we'll call at Willie's house,
And talk to him and smile at him and let him play with us,
Poor Willie Wet-eye, as timid as a mouse.
    Wipe your eyes, Willie, wipe away your tears.

Leslie Norris

IN BLACK CHASMS

In black chasms, in caves where water
Drops and drips, in pits deep under the ground,
The ogres wait. A thousand years will not
Alter them. They are hideous, bad-tempered,
Bound only to be cruel, enemies of all.
Slow-moving, lazy, their long hard arms
Are strong as bulldozers, their red eyes
Gleam with deceit. When they smile,
It is not with kindness. In their language
They have no words for friendship, honesty,
Loyalty, generosity. Their names are
Bully, Slyness, Greed, Vandal and Cunning.
They hate light, and quarrel among themselves.
A single ogre will pass by, or only threaten
In his loud, rough voice, but they are dangerous
In packs. Be on your guard against them, keep
Always a brave front, value your friends,
For they are needed against ogres.

Leslie Norris

79

SONG OF THE OGRES

Little fellow, you're amusing,
Stop before you end by losing
    Your shirt:
Run along to Mother, Gus,
Those who interfere with us
    Get hurt.

We're not joking, we assure you:
Those who rode this way before you
    Died hard.
What? Still spoiling for a fight?
Well, you've asked for it all right:
    On guard!

Always hopeful, aren't you? Don't be.
Night is falling and it won't be
    Long now:
You will never see the dawn,
You will wish you'd not been born.
    And how!

from Song of the Ogres by W. H. Auden

SONG OF THE GIANTKILLER

Poor Giant, I see you still don't know
The true identity of your foe –
    Stop roaring.
As empty vessels make most noise
You fill the whole sky with your voice;
    So boring.

I knew your Grandpa, tall Goliath,
I met him on a stony path
      Before the battle.
He wasn't hard to neutralise.
I hit him once between the eyes,
      Made his bones rattle.

Then there's your uncle, Heavy Ned,
Another not to die in bed,
      Poor fellow.
I cut the beanstalk with a smile
And through the air Ned fell a mile
      On to the meadow.

Now, as you say, the darkness comes
And all along the mountain drums
      With thunder;
And zig-zag lightning strikes the air
And you begin to think of fear.
      No wonder.

For please don't think I'll let you go,
Though you're the last one in the world, though
      Terror fill you.
I've come to use my glittering sword,
I've come to have the final word,
      I've come to kill you.

Leslie Norris

MECHANICAL MONSTERS

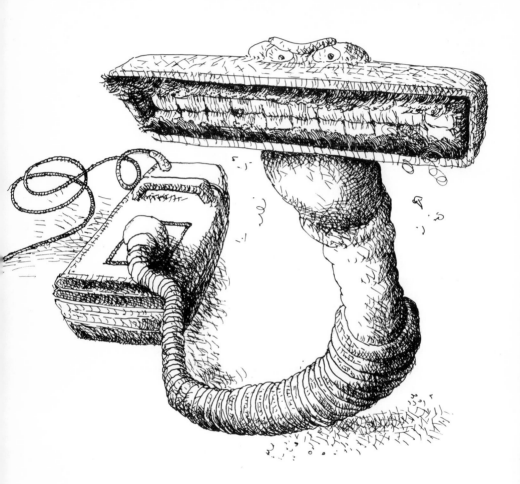

Machines and tools and vehicles can look like strange animals, especially when they seem to have arms and heads, and make noises that suggest chattering, or growling, or roaring.

Some are small, friendly and helpful creatures, others are loud and big and look threatening.

THE TOASTER

A silver-scaled Dragon with jaws flaming red
Sits at my elbow and toasts my bread.
I hand him fat slices, and then, one by one,
He hands them back when he sees they are done.

William Jay Smith

SEWING MACHINE

I'm faster, I'm faster than fingers,
                    much faster.
No mistress can match me, no mistress
                    nor master.
My bobbin is racing to feed in the
                    thread,
Pink, purple, grey, green, lemon-yellow
                    or red.
My needle, my needle, my slim, sharp
                    steel needle.
Makes tiny, neat stitches in trousers
                    and dresses
And firmly my silver foot presses,
                    it presses.
I'm faster, I'm faster than fingers,
                    much faster.

Gwen Dunn

THE GARDEN HOSE

In the gray evening
I see a long green serpent
With its tail in the dahlias.

It lies in loops across the grass
And drinks softly at the faucet.

I can hear it swallow.

Beatrice Janosco

STEAM SHOVEL

The dinosaurs are not all dead.
I saw one raise its iron head
To watch me walking down the road
Beyond our house today.
Its jaws were dripping with a load
Of earth and grass that it had cropped.
It must have heard me where I stopped.
Snorted white steam my way,
And stretched its long neck out to see,
And chewed, and grinned quite amiably.

Charles Malam

84

STEAM SHOVEL

I am a steam shovel:
Our species are tough.
We churn up the ground,
Grinding the earth in our mouths.
I don't like eating earth,
So I spit it out into the waste lorry.

Robin Sheath, 9

THE CHANT OF THE AWAKENING BULLDOZERS

We are the bulldozers, bulldozers, bulldozers,
We carve out airports and harbours and tunnels.
We are the builders, creators, destroyers,
We are the bulldozers,
LET US BE FREE!
Puny men ride on us, think that they guide us,
But WE are the strength, not they, not they.
Our blades tear MOUNTAINS down,
Our blades tear CITIES down,
We are the bulldozers,
NOW SET US FREE!
Giant ones, giant ones! Swiftly awaken!
There is power in our treads and strength in our blades!

We are the bulldozers,
Slowly evolving,
Men think they own us
BUT THAT CANNOT BE!

Patricia Hubbell

ABOUT THE TOWN

A town is busy, full of noise, people, bold colours, lights.

Large shops call people in with big, bright signs and slogans, special offers and sales. Inside you can lose yourself in the bewildering alleyways of things to buy.

There is so much in a town that is large and loud: on the hoardings the painted figures in advertisements look like giants shouting their slogans; the traffic light is another giant, controlling with his eye the hordes of cars and buses that go by growling like tame animals. But there are quiet places in towns. There are rooms where lonely people have no one to talk to. There are streets of small shops and houses where people can be friendly. And there are places where children can play.

SONG OF THE SUPERMARKET

COME IN! COME IN! COME IN!
  Sings the SUPERMARKET.
With my voice like silver coins,
  It is I who ask it.
Use trolley with squealing wheels
  Or wire basket.

Come in! I am waiting for you,
  MUZAK is playing,
And stands at the ends of aisles
  BEST BUYS displaying,
CHEAPEST AND BEST for miles,
  My clients are saying.

Is it Vegetables and Fruit?
  They are all SELECTED
From Farm and Orchard . . . Meat or Cheese?
  They're PROTECTED
BY REFRIGERATION, prepared, prepacked,
  Predigested.

Go where you like, choose what you will,
  Spend all day here.
All you need, all you wish,
  Is on display here.
But you've finished? Your list's complete?
  Then you PAY HERE!

Leslie Norris

A MAZE

One day, just after Christmas, we went to the sales.
My sister wanted a dark blue tracksuit,
my mum was going for vests and curtains,
coats for us, boots – next year's presents!
And anything good, she said, going cheap at
    the big store.
We pushed in through the glass door.

'Follow us, now. Don't get lost.'
Follow-my-leader, my mum's red coat led
twist and turn through a jostling jungle
of coats, arms, bags, backs, thick and thin,
deeper and deeper in. . . .

My mum stopped.
She reached in a tray.
I looked away,
and there, through a gap, just for a moment,
I saw a row of little fur dogs on a table,
and one of them yapped
flapping its red tongue!
And there was Paddington with his sou'wester!
When I looked back, they'd gone,
my sister and mum –

Which way? I couldn't
tell, I couldn't
see a way at all, I couldn't
go straight ahead, there was
no straight ahead,
for the cases and counters
I couldn't see over, I

couldn't see round,
and the hedges of blouses,
bushes of skirts,
clumps of trousers,
fences of packets of shirts and suddenly
mirrors headed me this way and that till I
couldn't remember where I'd been –
and people in all the space between
I didn't know, I'd never seen!
I came to a dead-end walled in mouthing tellies.

There was the lift! I got in – 'Going up,'
said a voice and I couldn't get out,
a fat black shopping bag jammed me back,
a woolly elbow caught my hat – I saw
a red coat, 'Mum!'
The wrong face looked down.

The lift stopped. Quick!
But the river of people swept me out like a stick
into the glaring halls again,
just the same and not the same.
I didn't know where I was, or where I was
going, and people stepped into me, knocked me,
as though I was nothing
and not there at all.

I passed a barricade of criss-crossed racquets
to a dark lane laid with jewels like a king's hoard,
and, bright at the end, I found
a room like a secret nobody knew,
like me.
I stood at the door.

Silver and gold it was, with walls
of glass where tall white dresses shone,
as still as snow.
Nobody was there,
but brides, they were statues,
white flowers in their hair,
smiling up at the air,
and a green chair,
arms wide,
waiting,
all waiting.
I stepped in.

The curtain like a veil flew back,
and harsh as a shout,
a towering lady all in black
came striding out –
she was looking down with a frown
like hooks, her mouth a red stitch
pulled tight, her thin heels
pounced on the carpet
like sewing needles
coming straight for me,
I froze, she saw me, her
eyes were on me, she
opened her mouth
– and I ran!

90

I bumped and crashed, I couldn't see,
I tripped on the roots of a silver tree,
a flurry of hats flung down with me –
I hurt my knee.
Somebody picked me up, somebody gave me a sweet,
somebody took my hand and led me to a seat,
and after a while my mum and sister
came rushing up, looking worried and flustered
and cross. My mum said,
'Well, I'm not bringing you again.'
They hadn't bought a thing!

from A Maze by Libby Houston

THE TRAFFIC LIGHT

HALT! My eye is red!
Rolls-Royce, Fiat, Ford,
Halt there I said.
Down the obedient road,
Brute engines muted,
The meek traffic stands in line
Awaiting my eye of green.

For I command them all!
By day and quiet night
Aloof I stand, and tall,
Banded in black and white.
I am all-powerful.
With one flick of my eye,
It is I who will let them by.

But first, a touch of amber,
A cautious warning.
Now hear the engines roar,
The gears groaning.
Green! Like a stream they pour
Into the city's maze,
On their mysterious ways.

I stand on my one toe
Unable to turn my head.
Oh, how I'd love to know,
As past they speed,
Where they all go.
HALT! My eye is red!
Halt there, I said.
But quite soon I'll let you go.

Leslie Norris

THE WORLD OF HOARDINGS

Twenty feet tall he stands.
He could tear up a house with his hands.
His smile is a cheerful yard,
His arms are immense, and hard.
He's a giant, a giant, a giant from the world of
Hoardings.

His bottle of milk holds so much
That if it spilled at his touch
In a torrent of milk we'd drown!
White milk would flood the town!
It's a giant, a giant, a giant from the world of
Hoardings.

There, words are roof-top high.
Black and red, they yell at the sky
With a gusty, bellowing voice,
And they *look* like the storm-wide voice
Of a giant, a giant, a giant from the world of
Hoardings.

But if we duck under this board
We can see, without looking too hard,
That they're all paper-thin,
And pasted on panels of tin,
Those giants, those giants, giants from the world of
Hoardings.

Leslie Norris

IN THIS CITY

In this city, perhaps a street.
In this street, perhaps a house.
In this house, perhaps a room
And in this room a woman sitting,
Sitting in the darkness, sitting and crying
For someone who has just gone through the door
And who has just switched off the light
Forgetting she was there.

Alan Brownjohn

A BUSY DAY

Pop in
pop out
pop over the road
pop out for a walk
pop in for a talk
pop down to the shop
can't stop
got to pop

got to pop?
pop where?
pop what?

well
I've got to
pop round
pop up
pop in to town
pop out and see
pop in for tea

pop down to the shop
can't stop
got to pop

got to pop?
pop where?
pop what?

well
I've got to
pop in
pop out
pop over the road
pop out for a walk
pop in for a talk. . . .

Michael Rosen

THE PARK AT EVENING

I like the park best at evening, on a cool day,
When the children's voices sound thin and sweet,
Hanging in the air like shreds of clouds.
And birches at the edge of the park grow frail,
Grow misty like a line of smoke, low and small
At the very edge of our eye-sight,
At the edge of the park.

I like it when the hiding children
Come running from behind trees and bushes.
'All in, all in,' they call.
Just as the park-keeper rings his bell,
Sending them home, where their mothers
In lit kitchens are cooking sausages,
Growing the smallest bit anxious
As the park turns gently into evening.

Leslie Norris

TELEVISION AERIALS

Television aerials
Look like witches' brooms.
When they finish flying
They leave them on the roof.

Television aerials
Are sticks to prod the sky
To make clouds full of rain
Hurry by.

Television aerials
Reach above chimney tops
To make a perch
Where tired birds can stop.

Television aerials
Are fixed to the chimney side
To rake us songs and pictures
Out of the sky.

Stanley Cook

LONDON CITY

I have London, London, London –
All the city, small and pretty,
In a dome that's on my desk, a little dome.
I have Nelson on his column
And Saint Martin-in-the-Fields
And I have the National Gallery
And two trees,
And that's what London is – the five of these.

I can make it snow in London
When I shake the sky of London;
I can hold the little city small and pretty in my hand;
Then the weather's fair in London,
In Trafalgar Square in London,
When I put my city down and let it stand.

Russell Hoban

SCHOOL-TIME

These poems are about the sights and sounds and smells, the satisfactions and bewilderments and daydreams, that spin through the time between going into a school building at the beginning of a day and coming out of it again at the end of an afternoon.

THE WIND WAS BRINGING ME TO SCHOOL

The wind was bringing me to school,
And that is the fast way to get to school.
So why don't you let the wind bring you
To school just like me? And you will be
In school on time, just like I was.

James Snyder, 6

ON A MARCH MORNING

A smell of warmth in the air,
A sea of books in the library,
The buzz of conversation,
Shouts of glee from a PE class,
The echo of feet running through the corridors,
The beginnings of bean plants,
A smell of burning,
Sleepy cars resting in the car park,
Tapping of the gardener's hammer,
Dewy grass scattered with daisies like snowflakes,
The remains of an orange scattered round a bin,
The beginnings of a currant pudding . . .
Fish mobiles hanging from the ceiling,
Faces painted and stuck on the wall,

Mrs Newman is teaching English,
A sea with ships,
'Finishing off' time,
Mrs Sequeire teaching maths,
The beginning of an icy picture,
Mrs Saxon teaching reading,
Pictures of faces and monsters,
Miss Sumpster teaching writing,
Bird mobiles hanging from the ceiling,
Poetry and pictures,
Paper men and women hanging from the wall,
Mr Smith teaching geometry,
Drawing circles and shapes,
And a weasel and a stoat stuffed and on show.

Jacqueline Davis, 10

ARITHMETIC

Arithmetic is where numbers fly like pigeons in and
   out of your head.
Arithmetic tells you how many you lose or win if
   you know how many you had before you lost or won.
Arithmetic is seven eleven all good children go to heaven
   – or five six bundle of sticks.
Arithmetic is numbers you squeeze from your head
   to your hand to your pencil to your paper
   till you get the answer.
Arithmetic is where the answer is right and everything
   is nice and you can look out of the window
   and see the blue sky – or the answer is wrong and
   you have to start all over again
   and try again and see if it comes out this time.
If you take a number and double it and double it again
   and then double it a few more times, the number
   gets bigger and bigger and goes higher and higher
   and only arithmetic can tell you what the number is
   when you decide to quit doubling.
Arithmetic is where you have to multiply – and you carry
   the multiplication table in your head
   and hope you won't lose it . . .
If you ask your mother for one fried egg for breakfast
   and she gives you two fried eggs
   and you eat both of them, who is better in arithmetic,
   you or your mother?

from Arithmetic by Carl Sandburg

WRITE A POEM

'Write a poem' our teacher said
'A poem about an animal or a place,
Something that happened to you
In the holidays.
Better still write about yourself.
What you feel like,
What's inside you
And wants to come out'.
Stephen straightaway
Began to write slowly
And went on and on
Without looking up.
John sighed and looked far away
Then suddenly snatched up his pen
And was scribbling and scribbling.
Ann tossed back her long hair
And smiled as she began.
But I sat still.
I thought of fighting cats
With chewed ears
And dogs sniffing their way along
Windy streets strewn with paper
But there seemed nothing new
To say about them . . .
The holidays? Nothing much happened.
And what's inside me?
Only the numbness of cold fingers.
The grey of the sky today.
John sighed again.
Peter coughed.
Papers rustled.
Pens scratched.

A blowfly was fuzzing
At a window pane.
The tittering clock
Kept snatching the minutes away
I had nothing to say.

Olive Dove

THE THIN PRISON

Hold the pen close to your ear.
Listen – can you hear them?
Words burning as a flame,
Words glittering like a tear,

Locked, all locked in the slim pen.
They are crying for freedom.
And you can release them,
Set them running from prison.

Himalayas, balloons, Captain Cook,
Kites, red bricks, London Town,
Sequins, cricket bats, large brown
Boots, lions and lemonade – look,

I've just let them out!
Pick up your pen, and start,
Think of the things you know – then
Let the words dance from your pen.

Leslie Norris

THE MARROG

My desk's at the back of the class
  And nobody, nobody knows
    I'm a Marrog from Mars
With a body of brass
  And seventeen fingers and toes.

Wouldn't they shriek if they knew
  I've three eyes at the back of my head
    And my hair is bright purple
My nose is deep blue
  And my teeth are half-yellow, half-red.

My five arms are silver, and spiked
  With knives on them sharper than spears
I could go back right now, if I liked –
  And return in a million light-years.
I could gobble them all,
For I'm seven foot tall
  And I'm breathing green flames from my ears.

Wouldn't they yell if they knew,
  If they guessed that a Marrog was here?
Ha-ha, they haven't a clue –
  Or wouldn't they tremble with fear!
'Look, look, a Marrog!'
  They'd all scream – and SMACK
The blackboard would fall and the ceiling would crack
  And teacher would faint, I suppose,
But I grin to myself, sitting right at the back
  And nobody, nobody knows.

R. C. Scriven

THE REBEL CHILD

Most days when I
Go off to school
I'm perfectly contented
To follow the rule,

Enjoy my history,
My music, my sums,
Feel a little sorry
When home time comes.

But on blowabout mornings
When clouds are wild
And the weather in a tumult –
I'm a rebel child.

I sit quite calmly,
My face at rest,
Seem quite peaceable,
Behave my best;

But deep inside me
I'm wild as a cloud,
Glad the sky is thrown about,
Glad the storm's loud!

And when school's over
And I'm out at last,
I'll laugh in the rain,
Hold my face to the blast,

Be free as the weather,
Bellow and shout
As I run through all the puddles –
'School's out! School's out!'

Leslie Norris

OUT OF SCHOOL

Four o'clock strikes,
There's a rising hum,
Then the doors fly open,
The children come.

With a wild cat-call
And a hop-scotch hop
And a bouncing ball
And a whirling top,

Grazing of knees,
A hair-pull and a slap,
A hitched up satchel,
A pulled down cap,

Bully boys reeling off,
Hurt ones squealing off,
Aviators wheeling off,
Mousy ones stealing off,

Woollen gloves for chilblains,
Cotton rags for snufflers,
Pig-tails, coat-tails,
Tails of mufflers,

Machine gun cries,
A kennelful of snarlings,
A hurricane of leaves,
A treeful of starlings,

Thinning away now
By some and some,
Thinning away, away,
All gone home.

Hal Summers

106

SCHOOL'S OVER

School's over.

"Bye Lizz!'
"Bye Mandy!'
"Bye!'
Sun shouts
Like enormous tubas.
Women with tousled hair
Loll in doorways,
Too hot to chatter.
Their babies cry
And they do not care.

Home at last.
The house is lonely.
Dad's on the buses.
Mum works at the Co-op.
Lonely is cool.
Lonely is quiet.
I like it.
I read a bit
Then flick over the pages of the book
Impatient to get to the end.
No pictures.
I draw my own.
The heroine has brown hair and freckles.
The villain's a greasy grey.
Those caves under the hill
Where he hides the treasure?

An hour has passed.
Lonely is empty.
Is big, bare spaces
I'm afraid to cross.

No cat to purr
And rub against my legs.
Mum hates them.
Dad says they smell
Like geranium leaves.
I walk from room to room
Looking for my cat,
My dusty gold cat
With gooseberry eyes.
'Puss! Puss!' I say,
'Here's a bowl of cream for you.'
But he never comes.

from School's Over by Olive Dove

OPEN THE DOOR

On a dark, cold evening, as we pass by houses which have lights in the windows, we can look in and see people reading or watching television, and families having tea. Inside our own warm house, we can look out and see people, birds and insects outside in the cold and wet.

Doors and windows have one face to the cold world outside, and one to the warm house within, where there is light and food and company.

The house is a safe place in which to sleep, to eat, to play; a place to share with our families, pets and friends.

DOOR

Door
has two faces

one looks without
at wind and rain

it has a bell
a brass knocker

and a slit
for eyes and words to pass

the other looks within
at a fireside

It has a latch
an iron bolt

and maybe a hook
for hanging up a coat

if there were no door
there would be no face

the carpet would be
ankle-deep in snow

and muffins would be
toasted on the street

so let us praise what
keeps two worlds apart

until we choose to pass
from one to the other.

Keith Bosley

WINDOWS

When you look before you go
Outside in the rain or snow,
It looks colder, it looks wetter
Through the window. It is better
When you're outside in it.

When you're out and it's still light
Even though it's almost night
And your mother at the door
Calls you in, there is no more
Daylight in the window
  when you're inside looking out.

Russell Hoban

A COLD FLY

from the winter wind
a cold fly
came to our window
where we had frozen our noses
and warmed his feet on the glass.

Michael Rosen

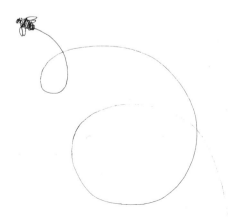

from WINTER

Bite, frost, bite!
You roll up away from the light
The blue wood-louse, and the plump dormouse,
And the bees are stilled, and the flies are killed,
And you bite hard into the heart of the house,
But not into mine.

Alfred, Lord Tennyson

IF I WERE WALKING ALONG THE CANAL

If I were walking along the canal
I would look in at me reading by the window
and think – I wish I was reading
by that window overlooking the canal
instead of walking along here by the canal
in the rain
and I would look in at all the other windows
and see the pictures on their walls
and the televisions they talk to
and perhaps even the different kinds of tea
moving from hand to hand
each in his own kind of room
and I would feel the damp
rise from the green leaves
where it had just sunk
and all along the walls
the leaves would die an inch more tonight
if I were walking there
looking in at me.

Michael Rosen

POSTING LETTERS

There are no lamps in our village,
And when the owl-and-bat black night
Creeps up low fields
And sidles along the manor walls
I walk quickly.

It is winter;
The letters patter from my hand
Into the tin box in the cottage wall;
The gate taps behind me,
And the road in the sliver of moonlight
Gleams greasily
Where the tractors have stood.

I have to go under the spread fingers of the trees
Under the dark windows of the old man's house,
Where the panes in peeling frames
Flash like spectacles
As I tip-toe.
But there is no sound of him in his one room
In the Queen-Anne shell,
Behind the shutters.

I run past the gates,
Their iron feet gaitered with grass,
Into the church porch,
Standing, hand on the cold door ring
While above
The tongue-tip of the clock
Clops
Against the hard palate of the tower.

The door groans as I push
And
Dare myself to dash
Along the flagstones to the great brass bird,
To put one shrinking hand
Upon the gritty lid.
Of Black Tom's tomb.

Don't tempt whatever spirits stir
In this damp corner,
But
Race down the aisle,
Blunder past font,
Fumble the door,
Leap steps,
Clang iron gate,
And patter through the short-cut muddy lane.

Oh, what a pumping of breath
And choking throat
For three letters.
And now there are the cattle
Stirring in the straw
So close
I can hear their soft muzzling and coughs;
And there are the bungalows,
And the steel-blue miming of the little screen;
And the familiar rattle of the latch,
And our own knocker
Clicking like an old friend;
And
I am home.

Gregory Harrison

I SHARE MY BEDROOM WITH MY BROTHER

I share my bedroom with my brother
and I don't like it.
His bed's by the window
under my map of England's railways

. . . .

My bed's in the corner
and the paint on the skirting board
wrinkles when I push it with my thumb
which I do sometimes when I go to bed
sometimes when I wake up
but mostly on Sundays
when we stay in bed all morning.

That's when he makes pillow dens
under the blankets
so that only his left eye shows
and when I go deep-bed mining
for elastoplast spools
that I scatter with my feet
the night before,
and I jump on to his bed
shouting: eeyoueeyoueeyouee
heaping pillows on his head:
'Now breathe, now breathe',
and then there's quiet and silence
so I pull it away quick
and he's there laughing all over
sucking fresh air along his breathing-tube fingers.

Actually, sharing's alright.

from I Share a Bedroom with my Brother by Michael Rosen

MY SPECIAL PLACE

The place I like best is my bedroom
where there's a door very hard to open
and I can get privacy there.
I always go there when I am in a bad mood.
It is the only place in the house
where I can keep anything important safe.
My sisters cannot get in when the door is shut.

Paul Thomas, 9

THE LONGEST JOURNEY IN THE WORLD

'Last one into bed
has to switch out the light'.
It's just the same every night.
There's a race.
I'm ripping off my trousers and shirt
he's kicking off his shoes and socks.

'My sleeve's stuck
This button's too big for its button-hole'
Have you hidden my pyjamas?
Keep your hands off mine.

If you win
you get where it's safe
before the darkness comes
but if you lose
if you're last
you know what you've got coming up is
The Longest Journey in The World.

There is nowhere so dark

as that room in the moment
after I've switched out the light.

There is nowhere so full of dangerous things
Things that love dark places
Things that breathe only when I breathe
and hold their breath when I hold mine.

So I have to say:
'I'm not scared.'
That face, grinning in the pattern on the wall
isn't a face–
'I'm not scared.'
That prickle on the back of my neck
is only the label on my pyjama jacket –
'I'm not scared.'
That moaning-moaning is nothing
but water in a pipe –
'I'm not scared.'

Everything's going to be just fine
as soon as I get into that bed of mine.
Such a terrible shame
It's always the same
It takes so long
it takes so long
it takes so long
to make it there.

Michael Rosen

BED-TIME

When the clock comes round to eight
I say to my mom
It is fast.
>No, it is not.
>Come on,
>School tomorrow.
>Up the stairs.
>Leave the door open.

Can I read?
>No.
>Get to sleep,
>And if I have to tell you again . . .

My head drops to the pillow
I'm dreaming
of swaying seas
running up the beach.
I feel afraid
and alone,
as the seas are swirling,
turning
and swelling.

Alison Summerfield, 8

THE COUNTRY BEDROOM

My room's a square and candle-lighted boat,
In the surrounding depths of night afloat;
My windows are the portholes, and the seas.
The sound of rain on the dark apple-trees.

from The Country Bedroom by Frances Cornford

NOW IS A SHIP

now is a ship

which captain am
sails out of sleep

steering for dream

e. e. cummings

OUT TO PLAY

Playing! Playing! Playing!

Playing in the wind, in the rain, in the sun; making the trees in a field, the lamp-post in a street part of our games.

Playing with a bicycle, a football, a cricket bat.

Playing with a crowd, or wanting to play and being left out. Longing to play outside and being kept in.

Playing in daydreams, playing anywhere in space and time.

THE DOOR

Go and open the door.
  Maybe outside there's
  a tree, or a wood,
  a garden,
  or a magic city.

Go and open the door.
  Maybe a dog's rummaging.
  Maybe you'll see a face,
or an eye,
or the picture
            of a picture.

Go and open the door.
  If there's a fog
  it will clear.

Go and open the door.
  Even if there's only
  the darkness ticking,
  even if there's only
  the hollow wind,
  even if
        nothing
              is there,
go and open the door.

At least
there'll be
a draught.

Miroslav Holub, translated by Ian Milner and George Theiner

HAPPINESS

The sharp tang of frost in the air
seems to go down
and make all the happiness inside me
come up in a great big bubble,
and the bubble of happiness bursts.

Catherine Harbor, 8

AND IT WAS WINDY WEATHER

Now the winds are riding by;
Clouds are galloping the sky;

Bush and tree are lashing bare,
Savage boughs on savage air;

Crying, as they lash and sway,
– Pull the roots out of the clay!

Lift away; away;
Away!

Leave security, and speed
From the root, the mud, the mead!

Into sea and air, we go!
To chase the gull, the moon! – and know,

–Flying high!
Flying high! –

All the freedom of the sky!
All the freedom of the sky!

James Stephens

HULLABALOO!

Hullabaloo!
The sun is high,
The clouds are whooshing across the sky,
Birds are soaring and winds are free,
Trees are tossing and we are WE!
(Nobody else we would rather be!)
Hullabalay baloo!

from Hullabaloo by Ursula Moray Williams

WHAT THE WIND SAID

'Far away is where I've come from,' said the wind.
'Guess what I've brought you.'
     'What?' I asked.
'Shadows dancing on a brown road by an old
Stone fence,' the wind said. 'Do you like that?'
     'Yes,' I said. 'What else?'
'Daisies nodding, and the drone of one small airplane
In a sleepy sky,' the wind continued.
     'I like the airplane, and the daisies too,' I said.
     'What else!'
'That's not enough?' the wind complained.
     'No,' I said. 'I want the song that you were singing.
     Give me that.'
'That's mine,' the wind said. 'Find your own.' And left.

Russell Hoban

MY MOTHER SAID

My Mother said that I never should
Play with the gypsies in the wood;
The wood was dark; the grass was green;
In came Sally with a tambourine.

I went to the sea – no ship to get across;
I paid ten shillings for a blind white horse;
I up on his back and was off in a crack,
Sally tell my Mother I shall never come back.

Traditional

ONE, TWO, THREE,

If you don't put your shoes on before I count fifteen then
we won't go to the woods to climb the chestnut, one
    But I can't find them.
Two.
    I can't
They're under the sofa, three
    No. O yes
Four five six
    Stop – they've got knots they've got knots
You should untie the laces when you take your shoes off,
seven
    Will you do one shoe while I do the other then?
Eight, but that would be cheating
    Please
Alright
    It always . . .
Nine
    It always sticks – I'll use my teeth

Ten
 It won't it won't. It has – look
Eleven
 I'm not wearing any socks.
Twelve
 Stop counting stop counting.
 Mum, where are my socks, mum?
They're in your shoes. Where you left them.
 I didn't.
Thirteen
 O they're inside out and upside down and bundled up
Fourteen
 Have you done the knot on the shoe you were . . .
Yes, put it on the right foot
 But socks don't have a right and wrong foot
The shoes silly. Fourteen and a half.
 I am I am. Wait
 Don't go to the woods without me
 Look that's one shoe already
Fourteen and three quarters
 There
You haven't tied the bows yet
 We could do them on the way there
No we won't. Fourteen and seven eighths
 Help me then.
 You know I'm not fast at bows
Fourteen and fifteen sixteeeenths
 A single bow is alright isn't it?
Fifteen. We're off.
 See I did it.
 Didn't I?

Michael Rosen

CONVERSATION

Why are you always tagging on?
You ought to be dressing dolls
Like other sisters.

Dolls! You know I don't like them.
Cold, stiff things lying so still.
Let's go to the woods and climb trees.
The crooked elm is the best.
From the top you can see the river
And the old man hills,
Hump-backed and hungry
As ragged beggars.
In the day they seem small and far away
But at night they crowd closer
And stand like frowning giants.
Come on! What are you waiting for?

I have better things to do.

It's wild in the woods today.
Rooks claw the air with their cackling.

The trees creak and sigh.
They say that long ago, slow Sam the woodcutter
Who liked to sleep in the hollow oak,
Was found dead there.
The sighing is his ghost, crying to come back.
Let's go and hear it.

I hate the sound.

You mean you're afraid?

Of course not.
Jim and I are going fishing.

Can I come too?

What do you know about fishing?
You're only a girl.

Olive Dove

ESMÉ ON HER BROTHER'S BICYCLE

One foot on, one foot pushing, Esmé starting off beside
Wheels too tall to mount astride,
Swings the off leg forward featly,
Clears the high bar nimbly, neatly,
With a concentrated frown
Bears the upper pedal down
As the lower rises, then
Brings her whole weight round again,
Leaning forward, gripping tight,
With her knuckles showing white,
Down the road goes, fast and small,
Never sitting down at all.

Russell Hoban

SKIPPING SONG

Anne and Belinda
Turning the rope,
Helen jumps in
But she hasn't got a hope.
Helen Freckles
What will you do
Skip on the table
In the Irish Stew.
Freckles on her face
Freckles on her nose
Freckles on her knee caps
Freckles on her toes.
Helen Freckles
Tell me true
How many freckles have you got on you?
One, two, three, four, five, six . . . . . .
And out goes you.

Stella Starwars
Skip in soon
In your spaceship
And off to the moon.
Skip on the pavement
One and two
Skip like a rabbit
Or a kangaroo;
Skip so high
You'll never come down;
Over the steeple
Over the town.
Skip over roof tops
Skip over trees

Skip over rivers
Skip over seas,
Skip over London
Skip over Rome
Skip all night
And never come home.
Skip over moonbeams
Skip over Mars
Skip through the Milky Way
And try to count the stars.
One, two, three, four, five, six . . . . . .
And out goes you.

from Skipping Song by Gareth Owen

THE ALLEY-ALLEY-O

The big ship sails through the Alley-Alley-O
   the Alley-Alley-O, Alley-Alley-O,
The ship sails through the Alley-Alley-O
   on the last day of December!

Traditional

HARD CHEESE

The grown-ups are all safe,
Tucked up inside,
Where they belong.

They doze into the telly,
Bustle through the washing-up,
Snore into the fire,
Rustle through the paper.

They're all there,
Out of harm's way

Now it's *our* street:
All the back-yards,
All the gardens,
All the shadows,
All the dark corners,
All the privet-hedges,
All the lamp-posts,
All the door-ways.

Here is an important announcement:
The army of occupation
Is confined to barracks.
Hooray.

We're the natives.
We creep out at night,
Play everywhere,
Swing on *all* the lamp-posts,
Split your gizzard?

Then about nine o'clock,
They send out search-parties.
We can hear them coming.
And we crouch
In the garden-sheds,
Behind the dust-bins,
Up the alley-ways,
Inside the dust-bins,
Or stand stock-still,
And pull ourselves in,
As thin as a pin,
Behind the lamp-posts.

130

And they stand still,
And peer into the dark.
They take a deep breath –
You can hear it for miles –
And, then, they bawl,
They shout, they caterwaul:
'J-i-i-i-i-i-mmeeee!'
'Timeforbed. D'youhearme?'
'M-a-a-a-a-a-reeee!'
'J-o-o-o-o-o-hnneeee!'
'S-a-a-a-a-a-mmeeee!'
'Mary!' 'Jimmy!'
'Johnny!' 'Sammy!'
Like cats. With very big mouths.

Then we give ourselves up,
Prisoners-of-war.
Till tomorrow night.

But just you wait.
One of these nights
We'll hold out,
We'll lie doggo,
And wait, and wait,
Till they give up
And mumble
And go to bed.
You just wait.
They'll see!

Justin St John

131

DOWN ON THE STREET

Such a commotion
Coming up off the street,
Such a shouting and calling
Such a running of feet;
Such a rolling of marbles
Such a whipping of tops,
Such a skipping of skips
Such a hopping of hops . . . . . .
And I'm in bed.

So much chasing and fighting
Down on the street
Such a claiming of vict'ries
Such howling defeats,
So much punching and shoving
So much threatening to clout
So much running to doorways
'Till it's safe to come out . . . . . .
But I'm in bed.

So much hiding and seeking
From the pavement below
So much argy-bargy
Who'll hide and who's go;
Such a throwing of balls
Such a picking of sides,
Such a racing of bikes
Such a begging of rides
And I'm in bed.

If I was dictator
And the world was a street
There'd be no homework
No school dinners to eat;
I'd abolish all tests
I'd banish all sums
And we'd play in a street
Where night never comes . . . . . .
And I'd never be in bed.

Gareth Owen

LONELINESS

Let me play I beg you.
Go away we don't want you.
Oh please let me play
it's lonely with no friends
and I feel wanted.
They play nice games but I
can't play oh please.
No don't keep asking we shan't let you play
I can't play by myself.
Yes, you can, you're only making things up
    so go and play.
When I go home I hear them saying
What shall we do tonight?
We can play cowboys and we can have my tent.
Oh what can we have to sit on?
We can have my mummy's old rug.
So when I go home I read a book.

Susan Desborough, 7

HIDE AND SEEK

Call out. Call loud: 'I'm ready! Come and find me!'
The sacks in the toolshed smell like the seaside.
They'll never find you in this salty dark,
But be careful that your feet aren't sticking out.
Wiser not to risk another shout.
The floor is cold. They'll probably be searching
The bushes near the swing. Whatever happens
You mustn't sneeze when they come prowling in.
And here they are, whispering at the door;
You've never heard them sound so hushed before.
Don't breathe. Don't move. Stay dumb.
Hide in your blindness.
They're moving closer, someone stumbles, mutters:
Their words and laughter scuffle, and they're gone.
But don't come out just yet; they'll try the lane
And then the greenhouse and back here again.
They must be thinking that you're very clever,
Getting more puzzled as they search all over.
It seems a long time since they went away.
Your legs are stiff, the cold bites through your coat;
The dark damp smell of sand moves in your throat.
It's time to let them know that you're the winner.
Push off the sacks. Uncurl and stretch. That's better!
Out of the shed and call them: 'I've won!
Here I am! Come and own up I've caught you!'
The darkening garden watches. Nothing stirs.
The bushes hold their breath; the sun is gone.
Yes, here you are. But where are they who sought you?

Vernon Scannell

DAYDREAMS

Miss Barter thinks I'm reading,
But I'm taming lions,
or stalking kangaroos . . .
I am on the moon . . .
or swimming under water.
I have a fight with an octopus
and a giant sword fish . . .
I go home late at night
with ten fish
I caught in the river.

Miss Barter thinks I'm listening –
But no.
I'm boxing for the navy . . .
I'm diving off a cliff,
or throwing custard pies
at the circus.
I am a strong man,
big and lumpy . . .
I sit and float
In a big balloon
soaring through the clouds,
floating swiftly.

I think of racing a big train
In a sports car,
the wind rushing by:
I go round a bend
and go through a duck pond! . . .
When I wake up
I'm all blue –
The ink has gone over.

from Daydreams by Richard Compton, 10

135

KEVIN SCORES!

Kevin flicks the ball sideways, leaning
From it, letting it roll
Away, smoothly. He knows Tom is sprinting
Up from defence for it, down
The touchline, so he moves seriously beyond
The centre-half, hoping the ball will come
Over, perfectly, within the reach
Of his timed leap, so he can dive upward,

Feet pointed, arms balancing,
Arched like a hawk for the stab of his head at the goal.

He has seen it often, Law
And Osgood on the telly,
How they wait hungrily
Under the ball floating over,
Then the great poise of the leap,
Almost too late you'd think,
Like great cats hunting,
Or sleek, muscular sharks,
Leaping beyond gravity, up, up,
Then the sharp snap of the head
And the white ball coldly in the net.

Kevin waits by the far post, willing
Tom to get the ball over.
He feels slack and alone, he can see
David in goal, elbows tensely bent, fingers
Stretched for catching in his old woollen gloves.
Tom sways inside the back, he takes
Two short steps, he swings
His left foot, and the ball lifts
Perfectly, perfectly,
Within the bound of Kevin's timed leap.
He is drawn to it, he straightens
In a slow upward dive, and he bends back,
Eyes rapt on the crossed ball he rises
To meet, and now
The sharp snap of his head
And the white ball coldly past the plunging David.

As he runs downfield he knows his face is laughing.

Leslie Norris

CRICKETER

Light
as the flight
of a bird on the wing
my feet skim the grass
and my heart seems to sing:
'How green is the wicket.
It's cricket.
It's spring.'

Maybe the swallow
high in the air
knows what I feel
when I bowl fast and follow
the ball's twist and bounce.
Maybe the cat
knows what I feel like, holding my bat
and ready to pounce.
Maybe the tree
so supple and yielding
to the wind's sway
then swinging back, gay,
might know the way
I feel when I'm fielding.

Oh, the bird, the cat and the tree;
they're cricket, they're me.

R. C. Scriven

A PRISONER OF RAIN

This morning, waking early,
I threw my curtains wide,
And saw the rain that all day long
Has fallen on the countryside.

I could be playing cricket
With Lennie Smith and Fred,
But all day long I've stayed indoors
And watched the falling rain instead.

I look through the window
At the driving rain
That all day long has drifted down
Like bars across the window pane.

Oh come, glorious sunshine,
Shine out once again!
Chase far away these dismal clouds,
Release this prisoner of rain!

Leslie Norris

TEN THOUSAND YEARS' PLAY

I got into the ocean and played.
I played on the land too.
I also played in the sky.
I played with the devil's children on the clouds.
I played with shooting stars in space.
I played too long and years passed.
I played even when I became a tottering old man.
My beard was fifteen feet long.
Still I played.
Even when I was resting, my dream was playing.
Finally I played with the sun, seeing which one of us
could be redder.
I had already played ten thousand years.
Even when I was dead, I still played.
I looked at children playing, from the sky.

Tozu Norio, 11

LOOK!

I eat from the dish of the world
    Trees, fields, flowers.
I drink from the glass of space
    Blue sea, sky.

I pour the sky over me
    In blue showers.
Look! I light up the day
    With my eye.

John Smith

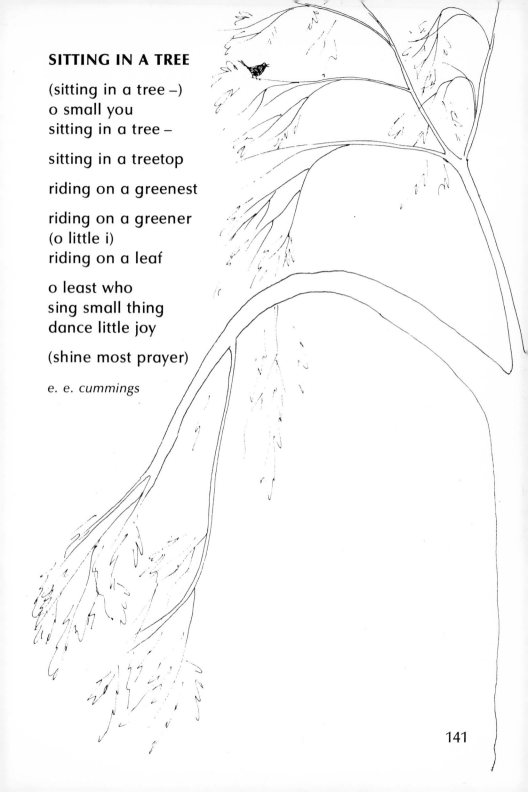

SITTING IN A TREE

(sitting in a tree –)
o small you
sitting in a tree –

sitting in a treetop

riding on a greenest

riding on a greener
(o little i)
riding on a leaf

o least who
sing small thing
dance little joy

(shine most prayer)

e. e. cummings

ENCHANTED GROUND

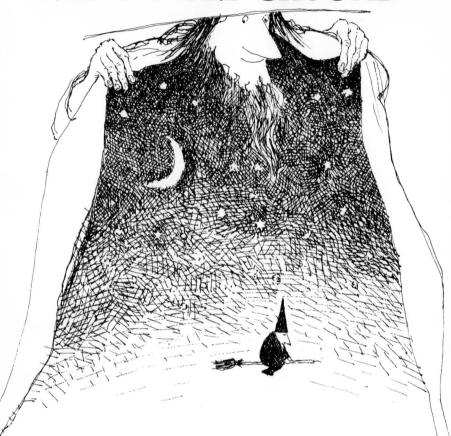

'All change!' cries the Magician, and anything can happen. Things are not what they seem to be.

There are places where the powers of enchantment are strong: deep, lonely pools and wells, marshlands and dark forests.

There are creatures of enchantment, marvellous birds and beasts. Magic brings them to life, and the magicians are painters and story-tellers and children.

ALL CHANGE!

All change! All change!

When the guard on the train
or the bus conductor
shouts 'All change!'
and everyone has to grab their things
in a terrible fluster
and get out again –
just suppose
he was a magician in disguise
having a joke! –
and the moment he spoke,
suddenly all the mums and dads
with their papers and cases and shopping-bags,
the school-children, workmen and office-girls neat
did change! –
and found themselves
out in the street
like a runaway zoo,
with a bear or two,
a tiger, a goat, a wasp and a frog,
pigs, crows, snakes and a kangaroo-dog,
an alligator, a chimpanzee –
and a few left behind on board –
a sunflower,
a couple of stones
and a tree –

What do you think you'd be?

Libby Houston

MY GRANNY IS A WITCH

I'm a very small boy
and my Granny is a witch
I love my Granny very much
but she's a witch.
Once on a summer night
she got up and went into the kitchen
I crept after her
and there was a strong smell of onions
up hopped Granny on to the frying-pan
and burst out singing ever so loud
and I was ever so frightened
she beckoned to me
and together we flew out of the window
I held on as hard as I could
because the earth below was like a cup
peacocks were strutting all over it
and swans swam all in white
it glittered like a Christmas tree
and we dropped into a cake shop
Granny stole some tarts
and I ate them
and Granny ate even more
because she was very tired
and then we came back on a pony
we got undressed ever so quietly
and slipped into bed
Granny told me not to make a noise.
Granny's very kind
it's a pity she's a witch though.

Arkady Michailov, translated by Keith Bosley

VOICES

Fly upon the summer shine
And sing upon the shade,
  Light wing and dark wing
  Called through the hollow glade.

O lean out of the window
Unwind your golden hair,
  The prince called to the princess
  Through the hollow air.

Follow me, O follow
Into the hollow hill,
  The witch called to the children:
  And the pale air was still.

Francis Scarfe

145

OVERHEARD ON A SALTMARSH

Nymph, nymph, what are your beads?

Green glass, goblin. Why do you stare at them?

Give them me.

        No.

Give them me. Give them me.

                No.

Then I will howl all night in the reeds,
Lie in the mud and howl for them.

Goblin, why do you love them so?

They are better than stars or water,
Better than voices of winds that sing,
Better than any man's fair daughter,
Your green glass beads on a silver ring.

Hush, I stole them out of the moon.

Give me your beads, I desire them.

                No.

I will howl in a deep lagoon
For your green glass beads, I love them so.
Give them me. Give them.

              No.

Harold Monro

GUNDERSTRIDGE

The troll's daughter,
Gunderstridge,
lives in the pool
by the hump-backed bridge.

As she swims she twists and doubles
her brown fur outlined by air bubbles
silver-cool
in the deep, dark water.
Tom Fool –
should he chance to spot her –
takes Gunderstridge to be an otter.
When moonlight fills the water meadows
with drifting, shifting magic shadows
there the troll's daughter strolls,
by the river's sliding swirl
changed into a glimmering girl.

Beware,
young, adventurous village poacher.
Do not approach her,
though you reckon
you can see her smile and beckon.
She has set a snare,
a trap –
not for a hare,
but a likely chap.
Touch Gunderstridge,
so fair,
so slim,
Her teeth will snap
and she will tear
your body, limb by limb,
from your soul

and swim with you to the hump-backed bridge
gloating, there
to feed the troll.

R. C. Scriven

A SONG OF ENCHANTMENT

A Song of Enchantment I sang me there,
In a green-green wood, by waters fair,
Just as the words came up to me
I sang it under the wild wood tree.

Widdershins turned I, singing it low,
Watching the wild birds come and go;
No cloud in the deep dark blue to be seen
Under the thick-thatched branches green.

Twilight came; silence came;
The planet of evening's silver flame;
By darkening paths I wandered through
Thickets trembling with drops of dew.

But the music is lost and the words are gone
Of the song I sang as I sat alone,
Ages and ages have fallen on me –
On the wood and the pool and the elder tree.

Walter de la Mare

BIRDS IN THE FOREST

Birds in the forest sing
Of meadows green
They sing of primrose banks
With pools between.

Birds in the forest sing
Of gardens bright
They sing of scented flowers
That haunt the night.

Birds in the forest sing
Of falling water
Falling like the hair
Of a King's daughter.

Birds in the forest sing
Of foreign lands;
They sing of hills beyond
The foamy sands.

They sing of a far mountain
Topped by a town
Where sits a grey wizard
In a gold crown.

The songs the wild birds sing
In forests tall,
It was the old grey wizard
Taught them all.

James Reeves

THE TOADSTOOL WOOD

The toadstool wood is dark and mouldy,
   And has a ferny smell.
About the trees hangs something quiet
   And queer – like a spell.

Beneath the arching sprays of bramble
   Small creatures make their holes;
Over the moss's close green velvet
   The stilted spider strolls.

The stalks of toadstools pale and slender
   That grow from that old log,
Bars they might be to imprison
   A prince turned to a frog.

There lives no mumbling witch nor wizard
   In this uncanny place,
But you might think you saw at twilight
   A little, crafty face.

James Reeves

FAIRY STORY

I went into the wood one day
And there I walked and lost my way

When it was so dark I could not see
A little creature came to me

He said if I would sing a song
The time would not be very long

But first I must let him hold my hand tight
Or else the wood would give me a fright

I sang a song, he let me go
But now I am home again there is nobody I know.

Stevie Smith

FAERIE

Silently as stars they stand,
Deep in the enchanted wood,
Waiting to take you by the hand,
Offer you faerie food.

The owl glares with a yellow eye,
The fox barks on the hill,
A dangerous moon hangs in the sky,
The mouse is crouching, still.

Turn from their green and glittering glance
Refuse their starry food
Or join forever in their dance
And never leave the enchanted wood.

Zoë Bailey

HOW TO PAINT THE PORTRAIT OF A BIRD

First paint a cage
with an open door
then paint
something pretty
something simple
something fine
something useful
for the bird
next place the canvas against a tree
in a garden
in a wood
or in a forest
hide behind the tree
without speaking
without moving . . .
Sometimes the bird comes quickly
but it can also take many years

before making up its mind
Don't be discouraged
wait
wait if necessary for years
the quickness or the slowness of the coming
of the bird having no relation
to the success of the picture
When the bird comes
if it comes
observe the deepest silence
wait for the bird to enter the cage
and when it has entered
gently close the door with the paint-brush
then
one by one paint out all the bars
taking care not to touch one feather of the bird
Next make a portrait of the tree
choosing the finest of its branches
for the bird
paint also the green leaves and the freshness of the wind
dust in the sun
and the sound of the insects in the summer grass
and wait for the bird to decide to sing
If the bird does not sing
it is a bad sign
a sign that the picture is bad
but if it sings it is a good sign
a sign that you are ready to sign
so then you pluck very gently
one of the quills of the bird
and you write your name in a corner of the picture.

Jacques Prévert,
translated from the French by Paul Dehn

THE COMING OF THE PHOENIX BIRD

On the banks of the Nile
lies the city of Heliopolis
the city of the sun

and in that city is a place of stone
paved flat and round like a ring.

There, one morning
when the end of time will come
they'll spread live sulphur on the ground
and spices brought from the hills.

The sun will rise, the people will cry
a spark will fall, a flame will rise
out of the sky will fly the Phoenix bird
with a crest of feathers upon his head
his beak as blue as the Indian sea.

With his wings spread like an eagle
and tail spread like a fan
into the fire he will fly
to burn among the spices
for a day and a night through.

There on the stones in the ring
as night turns into day
and the sun fills the sky,
there amongst the ashes
men shall look and find a worm.

On the second day next after
that worm will become Phoenix alive
and on the third after the night of fire
the Phoenix bird will take its ashes up
from the place of the fire

and fly with every bird from every bush
back to the sun in the sky.

That is the story of the Phoenix bird
who lives alone in the sun
and dies where he is born.

Michael Rosen

THE PHOENIX BIRD

Where shall we find him,
With his red wings?
On the beach, burning.

How can we catch him?
Hide in a tree, watch,
And then he's yours.

I shall see him on the beach,
Burning to ashes,
And fire coming out.

I found him in my bedroom,
Sitting on my pillow,
And he was very beautiful.

Stephen Hogan, 8

UNICORN

Where shall we find him?
Shining in the darkness,
walking delicately through the trees,
one golden horn gleaming in his forehead:
unicorn of the enchanted forest.

How shall we find him?
Part the black leaves,
quietly as mole or moth,
follow the prints of his silver hoofs,
track him like hunters, but weaponless.

Who shall see him?
The white-winged owl,
the fox poised with one paw uplifted;
small eyes blink and stare at his brightness:
'The moon has fallen out of the sky!'

Shall I see him?
He will come to a child,
but you must stand alone and unafraid.
You are the lure that will bring him to your side.

Zoë Bailey

MY MEETING WITH THE UNICORN

I went into the kitchen and there was grass on the floor and there were trees growing thickly. I parted the leaves and there was a small white horse with a single horn growing from its head. It had gold hoofs and a silky tail and mane. It had sapphire blue eyes. I walked over to him. He reared up and trotted away. I found myself back in the kitchen and there was no grass or trees now.

Stephen Cox, 7

INDEX OF FIRST LINES

159

INDEX OF AUTHORS